Praise for Gary Barker:

'The emotional heft of *The Museum of Lost Love* is obvious from the first page and never lets up. The characters breathe, they love, they mourn. They stay with you.'
JENNIFER FOX, Writer/Director/Producer of the award-winning film *The Tale*

'Gary Barker writes as beautifully and efficiently as any writer I've read—not an unnecessary sentence in the entire book. He is Hemingway without the false macho energy, and *The Museum of Lost Love* is an extraordinary testament to the enduring power of our pasts.'
RICHARD REYES-GAVILAN, Executive Director, Washington DC Public Libraries

for Mary of Kivu

'*Mary of Kivu* is the story of the Great African War, told with grace and passion. Drawing on his own experience in Congo and Rwanda, Barker depicts the horrors of war in an intriguing story that shows humanity's gift to forgive is greater than its genius to destroy.'
SHEREEN EL FEKI, author of *Sex and the Citadel*

'Barker writes with a simple, raw honesty that is captivating. No one is untouched by suffering in this novel. But the hope of healing and redemption, even in the darkest times, shines through. *Mary of Kivu* has an enduring, yet timely message: that forgiveness has the power to heal the deepest wounds—and create miracles in the process.'
KUWANA HAULSEY, author of *The Red Moon* and *Angel of Harlem*

GARY BARKER is an author, researcher, and human rights activist. He is founder and director of Promundo, an international organization that works with men and boys in more than twenty-five countries to achieve gender equality and end violence against women. He has been awarded an Ashoka Fellowship and an Open Society Fellowship for his work in conflict zones. His previous novels include *Luisa's Last Words*, *Mary of Kivu*, and *The Afghan Vampires Book Club* (co-written with Michael Kaufman). Barker lives in Washington, DC.

The Museum of Lost Love

Gary Barker

The Museum of Lost Love

WORLD EDITIONS
New York, London, Amsterdam

Published in the USA in 2019 by World Editions LLC, New York
Published in the UK in 2019 by World Editions Ltd., London

World Editions
New York/London/Amsterdam

Copyright © Gary Barker, 2019
Cover image © Diana Bejarano
Author portrait © Andy DelGuidice

Printed by Sheridan, Chelsea, MI, USA

Library of Congress Cataloging in Publication Data is available

ISBN 978-1-64286-042-9

Twitter: @WorldEdBooks
Instagram: @WorldEdBooks
Facebook: WorldEditionsInternationalPublishing
www.worldeditions.org

Book Club Discussion Guides are available on our website.

And love is not a victory march.
Leonard Cohen

Katia

Katia knew that look in her patients' eyes. She had questioned the competence of her own therapist. In her case it had been a woman, black like her, when she was fifteen. Now, as she started her own practice, the patients came to her instead. And she was convinced their lives were bigger and more damaged than her own.

She was silent as she sat across from her first patient of the day, a man about her age. He had short, tussled blond hair, his weathered skin affirming the hours he spent outdoors.

Katia wanted to throw her notepad at him: *Say something, will you?! This doesn't work unless you help me here.* This was their second session and both fidgeted as if on an internet-arranged date.

"Mr. Nielsen, how is your son adjusting?"

"You can call me Tyler. Mr. Nielsen sounds like my dad's name."

"How so?"

"I'm usually Officer Nielsen. Then I was Corporal Nielsen. But I've never really been Mr. Nielsen. Just Tyler."

"And now *you're* the dad."

"Sammy doesn't call me that."

"No, not yet, I'm sure. But he will."

Tyler stopped. He hunched his shoulders slightly as if confessing. This is how it went with him. He would start, stingily offer a few details, then stop again, staring at the floor or at his interlaced fingers. Seeing him like this, it was hard for her to imagine how he must have been when on patrol, with his uniform, his gun, his broad shoulders and muscular arms commanding respect.

Katia had asked her clinical supervisor about Tyler's long silences. *Just let him be. If it goes on too long, ask him again if he wants to continue seeing you. And if he says yes, let the minutes go. Ask some questions but not too many. If it goes on like that, I would say you stop the session after fifteen or twenty minutes and suggest to him that you start again the next week.*

Katia lost her concentration when he stopped like this. She thought about her recent move to Austin, her other clients, and whether Goran would call. Whether she wanted him to call. Whether she missed him. Or whether she was glad they were in this extended period of un-defined, long-distance whatever and that he was a safe distance away in the apartment they had once shared in Chicago.

"I'm worried about what I'm starting to feel and if it'll confuse him."

Tyler's voice seemed to come from the next room or the next building, from down the street. The words snaked their way into the quiet of the consultation room. It took Katia a moment to re-engage.

"What is it you're starting to feel?"

"For this woman I met. It's like my boy just came into my life. I never even knew I had a son until now. And just when I'm figuring out how to get on with him, I meet this woman."

"Do you want to talk about her?"

"It's not about her, or who she is really. It's about that feeling, if you know what I mean."

Katia knew she should wait for him to say more, but

the halting flow of Tyler's words was unbearable.

"Tell me about that feeling."

Tyler took a deep breath and stared at her with exasperation.

"It's like Afghanistan. Like being on those patrols. At night. Even with night gear and all. I mean even in the daytime in Afghanistan it's like you're blind. You have no idea when they'll hit you or what they'll hit you with or who's out there. If they're Taliban or just some goat herder and his family getting on with their day. Every time you come around a blind spot or a corner, every step, you're ready for that explosion. Direct or indirect. It's all the same. That's how I feel with a woman when I'm starting to care about her, you know. It's like love is ... like I'm completely blind."

Katia repressed a smile. Only occasionally did Tyler use so many words. She struggled not to hum the rest of the song that jumped into her head, and not to tell Tyler her own story. She knew that wasn't allowed, and she knew this wasn't about her.

"Sammy cries at night. He calls out for her, you know, for his mother."

"Does Sammy ever talk about her?"

"Not really. Only if I ask him."

"And, how do you feel about what Sammy's mother did?"

"I don't know what to make of it."

Katia waited again for him to say more but she did not insist. Neither did he say anything more about the woman he had just met. She let that go too. It was enough that he was using so many words. In the end, she was relieved that they had made it through this second session.

As Tyler closed the door to the consultation room,

Katia moved to her desk and opened her laptop. With one part of her brain she wrote up the notes from the session. The other part was thinking about that song. And that made her think about Goran.

Love is blindness. I don't want to see. Won't you wrap the night around me ... Oh, my heart. Love is blindness.

◆ ◆ ◆

"We should go here," Goran had said that morning, more than a year before Katia had moved to Austin. "We have a day in Zagreb before we leave for the coast."

They were sitting at the kitchen table in the small apartment near the university, where Goran worked. It still felt like his apartment, even though she had moved in with him a few weeks back. He handed her the *New York Times* Sunday travel section. Katia took a few minutes to read a short article describing the museum where people sent letters of love lost and ended.

"Sure, I guess. Sounds a little melancholic though," Katia said.

"We're a melancholic people," Goran said, smiling joyfully. He slid his right forearm across the small table to her right forearm and grasped gently. She felt safe like this, their arms interlaced, just as she had with every decision that had led her here, to move in with him.

They went back to reading their respective sections of the *Times*. He asked her if she wanted more coffee and he got up to make it. As he set her cup in front of her, he ran his fingers down her neck. It was one of things that had first attracted her to him, his long, elegant fingers. Katia turned the palm of his right hand up and kissed it and then pulled it under her robe.

This is what they could be. What they were. What she

imagined they would remain. She believed they were on a path that would take them from I-hardly-know-you to I-feel-like-I've-always-known-you. Katia had let go of her skepticism for long enough to believe that what they had was an open-ended parenthesis with no sign of closing.

Two weeks later they arrived in Zagreb late at night and checked into their hotel room, exhausted after the flights. Drifting into sleep, they rolled into each other in the middle of the sagging bed. It was late in the morning when she woke him up by running her hand along his arm. Her lips lightly touched his shoulder.

As they slowly emerged from their sleep, the only light was a thin white line coming through underneath the door. With her nose resting at the back of his neck, Goran's smell was familiar. Freshly cut wood mixed with a slight scent of sweat. This grounded her. She was glad the room had no distinct smell that distracted her from his.

They were mostly silent over what remained of the breakfast buffet in the ground-floor hotel dining area. All of it was pleasantly far from Chicago and from classes and term papers. Both could tell the other was enjoying being away from their daily routine.

They continued their silence as they walked the cobblestone streets through the upper, old city of Zagreb to the museum. Freed from their heavy winter coats, they held hands and let their arms sway as if they were only loosely connected to their bodies. The mid-morning air was comfortably cool, the sun shining with the promise of heat.

Goran looked at home here with his fair skin and straight, dark hair and a seriousness that in an instant could give way to his Balkan joviality. Katia, with skin the color of caffe latte and a long afro, stood out. They leaned into each other as they found the street where the hotel concierge had said the museum was, bracketed by a baroque church and a Greek orthodox seminary. Goran held the door open for her while still holding her hand. Normally Katia didn't like these overt displays of affection, but here she followed his lead.

He spoke in Croatian as he bought tickets from the young woman at the entrance. Then they stepped into a world of passion and love and sex gone wrong.

This was the place where the curators exhibited love's detritus. There were wedding dresses and keys and dolls and stuffed animals and dildos; objects of affections lost and ended through deception and confusion and death and migration and dozens of other reasons known, unknown, or unclear.

After reading several of the letters together, they went in different directions. Goran was drawn to a trunk and a smashed statue in a glass case:

He was never the same after the earthquake. It was as if all he thought he could build for me and build to keep us safe could be broken. He pulled away from me and could not talk. He could not get beyond speaking only the basic things he needed to communicate just to live. It was the gardener who saw him leave. He told me he saw my husband lean down to pick up the pieces of this statue. The gardener said my husband began to cry and then walked away. He did not come back. He wrote months later with an address of where to send some of his things. As if I had been nothing but a landlady, or the manager of a warehouse for his belongings, for our twelve years together. He didn't ask how I was. I didn't tell him that I was pregnant when he left. I didn't tell him about his daughter. He still does not know.

Kushiro, Japan, 2003

Katia was drawn to the corner with the sex toys, curious about the letters and stories that came with them. She read the letter next to a rabbit-shaped dildo:

We had seen each other at the pub on the corner near my flat and stopped to talk a couple of times. Then, that one Friday, we finally found ourselves sitting down for that drink we promised we would share one of these nights. It all happened without our having to say much. After drinks we went to my flat. She said the sex was amazing, that I was the first woman she had ever felt so free with. For that whole weekend we hardly got out of bed. I wondered if you could go crazy from amazing sex. I showed her my toys. She had this one in her purse. Then Monday came and we both had to go to work. I was sure when she called me at lunchtime that she would ask when we could get together again. That she missed me already. That she felt it too. She said I should know that she had a husband and that he couldn't know about any of this and that it couldn't happen again. She didn't ask for her dildo back.

London, England, 2007

Each story compelled Katia to read the next one, to understand and feel the love and the hurt that went into each letter and accompanying object. Some had videos and pictures, and at times Katia felt she was invading the privacy of all these lives—that the writers of these letters would somehow feel her peering into their secrets.

Katia was so engrossed in the stories that she was slow

to notice that Goran had been staring at the same exhibit for a long time. She became curious. Although she could only see Goran's backside, she thought she could tell by his posture that he was somber as he read.

Katia walked toward Goran, and said nothing as she came up beside him, casually placing her hand on his shoulder. She moved her hand up past his shirt collar to his neck. Under the glass and next to the letter there was a CD case and next to that a drawing of a house and garden that looked as if it had been done by a child.

Katia carefully read the letter.

We were together for just two days. Two days all those years ago. And I have never gotten him out of my head. It sounds trite even as I write it. He is my first love and he probably doesn't even know it. Our families were trying to get out at the same time. We were stuck in a transit camp, trying to leave at the beginning of the war.

It was very difficult to get out. You had to have papers in order, connections. Proof that no man in your family was running away from being drafted. Proof that you had somewhere to go. That some country, one not falling to pieces, would accept you.

We stayed up late into the night, all night, telling stories about our friends, our families, and our schools. He was fourteen. Nearly fifteen, he insisted. I was sixteen. He was so sweet, and so nervous. I could tell he had probably never talked like this with a girl before. He said he was sad that he had to leave his guitar behind.

He had a portable CD player with earphones and when we ran out of things to talk about, he put one earphone in my ear and the other in his and we listened to his CDs together. With his fingers he tapped the rhythm on my leg, pausing the CD and going back to lyrics that he wanted me to understand. His English was much better than mine and I could tell that he enjoyed being able to translate for me.

I took out the notebook I had in my backpack and showed him a drawing that I had made when I was younger of the cottage my grandparents had outside of Mostar. The notebook was one of the few things I was able to bring, apart from my clothes.

He saw me getting sad when I talked about the cottage, and about my grandparents, who were not going with us. He looked at me for a long time. Then he brushed the hair out of my eyes and ran his hand along my cheek. He moved his arm so our forearms were entwined. Then he brought his mouth to mine.

I wonder if he remembers that kiss. It was a kiss that carried my whole body with it. And I wonder if he remembers how safe he made me feel when he held my arm like that.

I wonder where he is now. His family was going to the US.

I wonder if he ever stays awake at night thinking about that kiss the way I do. I wonder if he knows that was the last time I felt safe.

Almost every day I wonder what has become of him. Whether he has children. Whether he is married. What he looks like as an adult. What kind of man he turned into. What his life is like.

This is all I have of that time: the drawing I did of my grandparents' cottage and the CD he gave me to remember him by. U2's *Achtung Baby*. Everybody liked "One" but he liked "Love Is Blindness." He played the song for me, and read me the lyrics as if reciting a poem he had written himself.

I tried to give him the drawing of my grandparents' cottage as my gift to him, but he refused. He said that the house might not be there when I came back after the war and that the drawing might be my only way to remember.

For a moment he sounded so wise, much wiser than the fourteen-year-old boy that he was.

In the end he was right. My grandparents' house did not survive the war.

He and his family made it out the next day. Mine never did.

Maybe I am sending this to see if he will find me. Mostly I think I am sending it so I will forget. Or at least think about him in a different way. In a way that doesn't keep me awake at night. Or maybe I'm just sending these things because I don't need them anymore.

Novi Grad, Bosnia and Herzegovina, 1992,
and Toronto, Canada, 2010

Katia thought she could hear two voices in her head: the voice of the young girl in the transit camp, and the voice of the adult woman looking back. She imagined herself having coffee with this woman, asking her about her life since the war and about the young man in the transit camp, whose family had left Bosnia around the same time Goran's had.

Katia looked at him. Goran did not return her gaze. His eyes were focused on the CD cover. She saw that he was crying. It was endearing that Goran would be so moved by this, yet she knew him well enough to know that he was not easily driven to tears. Katia followed his eyes to the CD.

It was marked with initials. In a handwriting Katia had come to know, from notes left in her mailbox, or on the grocery list stuck to the refrigerator in the apartment, she saw the letters. GV.

Her GV. Goran Vukovic.

"Goran," she said.

He did not answer.

"Goran?" she said again. "Is she talking about *you?*"

There was no reason to be jealous or insecure. Her tone was from curiosity and amazement that he, her Goran, would be part of this museum. And part of this woman's life, and that this story had found him here, like this.

Goran started to answer. He turned to face Katia and she took her hand off his shoulder.

"Katia ... I ..." he started, his voice struggling to restrain emotion. "I had no idea this was here."

"Goran, it's amazing that this found you. You've never been in touch with her?"

He turned away from her.

"No, no, of course not. I had no way to find her and I didn't even think she remembered. That was such a long time ago. I ..."

Katia reached out gently with both of her hands to hold Goran's arm: "You made her feel safe ..."

Goran pulled his arm away and stared at her.

"It was more than that. It was the middle of a fucking war. People were doing anything to get out. You don't know what that was like. We knew what they were doing to women and girls. Her family didn't get out."

"No, I guess I don't understand. I didn't live through the war."

"No, you didn't."

"Take your time, Goran. I'll wait for you in the café."

His look told her he was relieved to have a moment to himself. She walked out the exit and entered the lobby.

From across the small gift shop, Katia watched other visitors coming into the museum. In the gift shop she glanced at the various objects for sale, all with designs featuring broken hearts and fractured lines. After another group of visitors entered and paid, Katia felt the woman who sold tickets looking at her. Whether here or back in the US, she was used to such stares.

"You have beautiful hair," the woman said in slightly accented English.

"Thank you," Katia replied.

She gave a quick, false smile to the woman, looked down, and then walked to the museum café and sat at a table in one corner. The waiter, a young man dressed in black pants and a black T-shirt, offered her a menu, and took her order.

While she waited for her coffee, Katia ran her finger around each of the buttons of her sweater, starting at the top and working down and then back up. She ordered a second double espresso. Although her back was toward the exit of the exhibition space, she could sense Goran walking toward her. She felt his hesitation. He knew that Katia wanted to know more about the girl in the camp. But even more, that she wanted to know why he had reacted that way.

◆ ◆ ◆

As Katia finished typing up her notes from her session with Tyler, she looked at her mobile phone. No missed calls, no texts.

With each day away from Goran she was learning this: the normal state of lovers, of couples, is not together. Together is a transient state. The normal state of things is as much about ending and leaving as it is about beginning and staying. The normal state of love is living with the possibility that everything can, at a moment's notice, come tumbling down. We impossibly walk for some amount of time in the same pages, in the same narrative, and we deny with every breath the possibility, indeed the likelihood, that the arc of the story bends toward being alone.

Every city, Katia thought, every village, every neighborhood, should have a museum like the one Goran had taken her to visit more than a year ago. Children should be given classes in how to break up and move on. How to mourn the sudden loss of all-encompassing love or the end of an intense, fleeting affair and carry on with dignity. How to let someone get that close, know you that way, and let them go, taking with them your secret words and bedroom stories and those private little cries and tremors. How to walk into the story with kindness, and walk out of it without drawing blood.

Sometimes, when Katia found herself missing Goran and wondering what might be next, she looked at her phone and scrolled through the pictures she had taken of the letters and objects in the museum. Someday, she thought, she might submit one.

MUSEUM SUBMISSION 23-2006

We met at a tattoo parlor in the Village. We were there with mutual friends. The deal was that we were all going to get one. He could see I wasn't sure. He whispered in my ear, asking if I wanted to make a run for it. He texted an excuse to our friends that I wasn't feeling well. Once we were outside he grinned at me like he was five-year-old boy.

We stayed up all night just talking. How many guys really say what they feel? And then there was how he reacted when he saw my left hand. I was born with just four fingers on that hand. It's always curious to see how people react. I like to watch them squirm when I catch them counting a second time. Not him though. He just held my hand and said that he always thought nine was a much more interesting number than ten. His mother was a pediatrician so he even almost knew the proper name of my condition: Symbrachydactyly.

He called a few weeks later and said that he had broken up with his girlfriend and that he wanted to see me. I told him we should give it some time. He said that it had already been some time since we met at the tattoo parlor and that he had been thinking about me ever since.

We met at a coffee shop near my dorm. From then on it was like every moment between classes, we just wanted to be together. It was two months later that he said he loved me and I said it back, which is not a thing I do, ever.

We started doing things couples do together. He met my father, who took us out to dinner when he passed through the city. We hung out with each other's friends. But I never met his parents.

Three months later he went to a journalism seminar at Kent State with two other classmates. They rented a car and on the way back they were hit by a truck that had jumped the median.

I totally lost it. I cried for days.

I didn't get an announcement about the funeral. His roommate told me when it was and we took a train together to Philadelphia. After the ceremony there was a gathering at his parents' house. I didn't want to go, since I wasn't invited, but his roommate insisted.

His parents asked me how I knew their son. Before I answered, his mother reached out to hold my hands. She could see my sorrow, or see something, I think. As she held my hands, she looked at my left one for a few seconds. But I don't think she figured it out.

I told her I was their son's girlfriend and they both looked at each other awkwardly. Just then, a young woman came over to us. I recognized her. It was his previous girlfriend, the one he had broken up with to be with me.

His ex went up to them and they hugged her. She and I made eye contact and I just nodded and walked away while the three of them hugged and cried.

I started to leave the house but then I snuck upstairs and found his room. I saw the young him. I imagined we might have slept together in his teenage bed. I took this, this trophy, from a high school tennis tournament, and I put it in my purse.

If his parents ever come to the museum and say it's theirs, you should give it to them. They knew him longer. Their tears weigh more than mine. Although I do think that waking up with him next to me and hearing him say he loved me means something. That gives me some rights, doesn't it? Even if they don't know who I am. Even if his mother didn't notice how many fingers I have.

New York City, USA, 2006

Tyler

Tyler looked at the sleeping boys next to him. One shared his sandy blond hair, crinkly eyes, and surfer-boy softness. The other had wavy dark hair and dark eyes that reminded Tyler of the boy's mother. When they were awake, it was all he could do to keep up with them. When they slept, he tried to pull himself together.

Where the Wild Things Are was open at the foot of Tyler's bed. There were two matchbox cars on his nightstand. Sammy had wanted Tyler to read the story, while Joaquin had insisted on driving the matchbox cars over Tyler's bed. Joaquin had pretended not to listen to the story but Tyler could tell that he had been fascinated by it. Before Tyler reached the last page, both boys were yawning. Tyler let them fall asleep in his bed, and then he took them one by one to their beds in the room they shared.

Before the boys came to live with him, Tyler had never felt time shift so acutely. This was the only moment in the day when his apartment was quiet. These two bodies of perpetual motion collapsed and a parallel universe opened up. In that space Tyler had time to think, to recollect, to regret. He felt relief when he, too, could sleep.

Most nights, as he crossed over into sleep, Tyler's last conscious moment was one of longing—for warm skin touching him and a mouth close to his. It didn't surprise him when a short time later his sleep was interrupted by one of the boys, or both, calling for a glass of water, or, more often, crying out for their respective mothers. He understood their cry, shared it even. Still, no matter how quickly he reached their room in response to their cries, he was an impostor parent.

This new life had started with a phone call less than a year before.

Tyler, it's me. Melissa.

Melissa. It's been a long time. How um ... Where are you? Are you back in Austin?

Yes, visiting. I want to see you. I have something to tell you.

...

It's not what you think.

...

I heard you made it back from Afghanistan in one piece. I mean, unless you have PTSD or something.

No, I'm okay. I think. But thank you for asking.

Can I come over? There's someone I want you to meet.

...

It's your son.

Jesus, Melissa. Shit, why didn't you tell me?

And why didn't you tell me you were joining the army, Tyler?

Melissa, you wrote me off long before I enlisted. If I had known ...

Tyler, I told you I wasn't looking for anything when we met.

And so you couldn't even bother to tell me you were pregnant, and had ...?

Look, Tyler ...

Shit, I can't believe you waited all this time to tell me.

...

...

You still with me, Tyler?

Yeah.

So are you back at being a cop?

Yeah. Bastrop County Sheriff's Department.

You got a girl? Some good Christian lady you can take home to meet your momma?

No, Melissa, there's no one at the moment, good Christian or otherwise.

Where are you living?

I've got an apartment in Bastrop. The county gave me one.

The county gave you one? What, are you on welfare or something?

It's an apartment complex where battered women and their children live. County supports it. Run by the family crisis agency. They give me the apartment for free. Need a cop around. Makes the women feel safer. You know, just in case any of the guys try to come look for them.

Wow. There's got to be a word for that. Lots of mistreated, lonely women and a hot, single cop. What would that be? Supply meets demand?

Can I meet him, Melissa?

That's why I called.

It was Friday and he didn't have patrol that weekend. As he hung up, the first thing he thought about was what four-year-old boys liked to eat. This was something he learned to do in Afghanistan. When that out-of-control feeling came over him, those moments on patrol when an IED or an ambush might be around the next corner, he learned to focus on something small, something obvious. A task to complete.

The next morning Melissa brought Sammy over. Tyler had thought about proposing that they meet at the park by the river, or at a coffee shop, but he wasn't sure he wanted to see his son's face for the first time with strangers around. He wasn't sure how he would react, or how he was supposed to act.

Melissa rang from the front gate of the apartment complex and Tyler buzzed them in. He heard the knock at the door and stood up. He looked around his simple, mostly undecorated apartment to make sure it was presentable to a four-year-old, and to Melissa.

Tyler opened the door. Melissa wore a tropical print dress. His eyes were drawn to her tan neck. He remembered resting his head there. She leaned in to kiss him on the cheek. Melissa smelled much the same as he remembered, like sandalwood. Tyler thought he could smell pot on her breath.

"You look good," she said. "You can still break hearts. I bet the women here don't mind having you around."

Their gazes turned at the same time to Sammy, who was closely examining a Big Wheel outside an apartment two doors down from Tyler's.

"Sammy, come meet Tyler. This is who I told you about. He's your daddy. Remember what we talked about?"

Sammy lingered for a moment near the Big Wheel and then walked towards them.

Tyler felt a flush of his skin, like a first kiss or that moment when a girl he liked suddenly noticed him. That was the only feeling that came close to this. He felt Sammy's eyes on him, but even more so he felt a stare from Melissa, a look that he could not understand.

He bent down and extended his hand. Sammy looked at him with a serious but calm face and shook it.

"So, Sammy, I'm Tyler. I'm really happy to meet you. I really am. I didn't …"

"Can we come in?" Melissa asked.

"Yes, of course. Come on in. I got some juice and cookies for Sammy."

Sammy part-hopped, part-jumped, part-walked in, and began to inspect the apartment. He saw Tyler's guitars in their stands and walked over to one of them.

"Be careful with those, Sammy," Melissa said.

"It's okay. You can touch them if you're careful," Tyler said.

Sammy strummed one of the guitars and wiggled in response to the sound.

"Can you play something?" Sammy said, looking back at Tyler.

Tyler picked up the closest acoustic guitar and started to pick *Blackbird* by the Beatles.

Sammy smiled and Tyler smiled back.

"Do you like to draw?" Sammy asked, looking at Tyler.

Tyler stopped playing.

"Don't get too excited, Tyler. Every three-year-old on the planet likes to draw," Melissa said.

"I'm four," Sammy said.

"Of course, I know, honey."

"Yeah, I do like to draw," Tyler said. "Hang on a second and I'll get some paper and pencils and we can both draw."

Tyler left the room and returned with a wooden art case that he set on the floor and opened in front of Sammy. Sammy stared, transfixed at the dozens of colored pencils and the paper and the drawings that Tyler pulled out from the case.

"You're a good draw-er," Sammy said.

Tyler opened up a drawing pad for Sammy.

"Do you like pencils, or crayons, or pastels ...?"

"Yeah," Sammy said and picked up a blue pencil.

A few minutes later, with the two of them engrossed in drawing, Melissa stood up.

"Hey, you two. I need to go to the pharmacy to get

something, okay? I'll let you two get acquainted. I'll be back in a little while."

As she closed the door, Tyler stopped drawing long enough to think that it was a little strange that she was leaving Sammy alone when he and Tyler had only just met.

They continued drawing. Later, Tyler made them both sandwiches, and then he played guitar again and he showed Sammy how to strum while he held the chords. Then they drew some more, taking turns finishing each other's drawings.

"My mommy's not coming back," Sammy said calmly, his gaze on his drawing. His voice had an unusual weight for a four-year-old.

"Of course she is, but we'll have fun until she does. And even after you and your mommy leave, you can come see me anytime you want and I'll go see you too."

"Nope, she's not coming back."

"I'm sure she is. Your mom probably just got delayed. I can call her."

"Mommy told me she wasn't coming back. Mommy said you were going to take care of me for a while," Sammy said, still not looking up from what he was drawing.

Tyler had his mobile phone in his hand and was getting ready to dial her number. Sammy had looked up from his drawing now and was staring at him. Tyler was surprised at how calm Sammy was in stating that Melissa would not return. Tyler pulled up recent calls and dialed the number Melissa had used to call him. A message informed him that the number did not accept incoming calls. Tyler tried not to show any expression to Sammy as he called the number a second and a third and a fourth time. Then he texted a message to the number and immediately received a response: *Error: invalid number.*

They drew and watched TV until it was time for dinner. Tyler suggested they go out for dinner and Sammy vigorously shook his head.

"I need my car seat," Sammy said.

"Oh, yeah, of course. Well, I'll tell you what. You sit in the back seat and we'll put on your seat belt. I'll drive slowly. I'm a policeman, so it'll be okay just this once. I give you permission."

Sammy nodded his head, apparently satisfied with this.

On their way back to Tyler's apartment after dinner, Sammy was nearly falling asleep. As they walked inside, Tyler suggested he take a nap until Melissa came back.

The nap became a full night's sleep. Tyler watched Sammy as the boy slept on his couch until after two in the morning. Then Tyler took off his own shirt and shoes and went to his bedroom and slept on top of the covers of his bed. It was about seven the next morning when he woke up and saw Sammy standing next to him in his bedroom.

"I told you she wasn't coming back."

"Hey," Tyler said, his voice groggy. "We'll figure it out."

"Can I have some cereal?"

With more than four years having passed since they had broken up, two tours of duty in Afghanistan, and both of them moving to new cities, Tyler had no other current phone numbers for Melissa. She had made it clear when she ended it that she didn't want to stay in touch. She never told him where she had moved, although he thought it might have been the Bay Area in California.

She had friends there, and a cousin she was close to, and she had sometimes talked about moving there.

After taking four days of sick leave, buying a car seat, finding a temporary babysitter, contacting Child Protective Services, calling his mother in Houston with the news, asking her to take a few days off work to come stay with him to help get Sammy settled in, filling up his refrigerator with food Sammy liked, and buying clothes and a mattress for Sammy to sleep on, Tyler remembered the name of one of Melissa's close friends. It was one he thought lived in California. With a little online searching, he found a telephone number and a picture online that matched what he recalled the woman to look like.

"Ashley, I'm not sure if you remember me but this is Tyler Nielsen. I was Melissa's boyfriend for a while. I don't know if you've seen her recently but she has a son, I mean *we* have a son ..."

"Yeah, I know about that."

"Listen, Ashley, Melissa left Sammy with me and then just disappeared. I live in Bastrop, near Austin. I don't know if this was something she planned, or if something happened to her, or if she's been in touch with you. I'd never even met him. I didn't even know about him and she just left him here with me. Sammy says she told him that she was going to leave him to live with me, which seems to me about the craziest ..."

She cut him off: "Tyler, I can't tell you anything more. She made me swear that I wouldn't. You're a cop, aren't you? I mean, couldn't you find her if you really wanted to? Don't you have ways of tracking people down? Credit cards, phone numbers? Doesn't sound very smart to leave your kid with his father who is a cop and think you can disappear without being found."

"I guess not," he finally said. "Unless you figure the

guy is smart enough to know that you can't make a woman be a mother to a child if there's some reason she doesn't want to."

"You know, Tyler, she always said one of the reasons she liked you was because of your—what did she call it? —your 'simple, decent common sense.' So glad I could be of help. Good luck. I really mean that."

"Yeah, ok," he said, slowly taking this in.

He was about to hang up when Ashley spoke again.

"Tyler, hold on a second. Look, we tried to talk her out of it. I think it's a stupid idea. But she thinks you can do this. She has her reasons. That's all I can say."

He waited, thinking she might offer more information, a motive, something to go on.

"Take good care of Sammy," Ashley said.

Tyler thought it sounded like a threat. She hung up before he could respond.

About a week later Tyler received a registered letter. Inside was Sammy's birth certificate, listing Tyler as the father, a notarized letter signed by Melissa saying that she relinquished sole custody of Sammy to him, and Sammy's vaccination records. Tyler knew there would be more paperwork, meetings with social workers, and a court hearing to make it all permanent. The therapy was his own choice.

MUSEUM SUBMISSION 71-2005

She was working as a volunteer at an NGO in Rio de Janeiro. We were together for nearly a year. She moved into my apartment and got her visa renewed so she could spend more time in Brazil. Marriage really never came up, but we knew it was one way for her to get a permanent visa.

It was the first time we had spent Carnaval together in Rio. I tried to explain to her that crazy things happen. Like why do you think the government distributes condoms by the tens of thousands every Carnaval? There's the heat and the drums and beer and caipirinhas and bodies and we know what's on everybody's mind. It's not a normal time. When I told her this she looked at me in one of those lost-in-translation moments.

So this girl came up to me when we were at the Sambodromo and started dancing right next to me. Then she put her mouth to my ear and said she had been in a class with me at university. I didn't remember her, but maybe she was. She kind of looked familiar. When I turned to respond, she started kissing me. And then I found that I was kissing her back and she pulled me to her and grabbed my ass and maybe I grabbed hers. For a minute I forgot about my American girlfriend standing right beside me.

That's Carnaval. That's what I'd tried to tell her.

I don't know how much time passed. When I turned I saw my girlfriend take off through the crowd. I went after her but I couldn't find her. It's like thousands of people. I tried calling her mobile but she didn't answer. I went back to where we were sitting and waited but she didn't return.

She came back to my apartment two days later.

I asked if she was okay and she started kissing me and told me she was sorry and it didn't matter and would I forgive her no matter what she did and pretty soon we were on the floor taking each other's clothes off.

Later that same night, she packed and left. She wouldn't tell me anything else. Where she was going, anything.

This is the condom package and the flyer they handed out that year at the Sambodromo. It was the health ministry's way of getting back at the Catholic Church, which said that condoms promoted infidelity and promiscuity. The condoms came with this drawing of a friar, a nun, and a devil, that says: "Beyond good or evil, use condoms."

I wrote her emails: two or three a day for weeks. Short ones: *Write me, please. Please, I want to talk.* Or: *I miss you.* Or, some days: *I love you.*

Sometimes I wrote longer ones. She never wrote back.

Rio de Janeiro, Brazil, 2005

Goran

The transit camp was set up in a primary school about two kilometers outside the center of the small town. Teachers had been replaced by guards. Or maybe, Goran thought, the male teachers and staff had simply become the guards. The men in charge were standing in small groups, smoking, rifles hanging on their shoulders. Mostly they laughed. Until someone approached the gate from inside or outside. Then they immediately turned serious. And the rifles came off their shoulders and into their hands.

Goran's mother was inside, in what had been the school's office, waiting to show their papers. A line of adults, backpacks on their shoulders and suitcases at their feet, extended outside and part way around the building.

On their first day in the camp, Goran and his younger brother Srdjan played football with other boys their age. There were Bosnian Serbs, Serbs, Bosniaks, and Catholic Croatians, as there always had been in Yugoslavia. Later that same day, Goran joined the group that was playing basketball on the outdoor court. They asked around where each was trying to go.

Germany, the US, Croatia for the Croats, Slovenia would do, Austria, the UK, Canada. One said Russia. The others laughed.

"That's just trading one mafia state for another," one of them said.

The rest of the time, Goran sat on a table outside reading and listening to his CD player, hoping his batteries would last.

His mother had no news at the end of the day.

"They just need to check a few things. The people inside are nice. We should be allowed out in a day or two."

Her face was tense. Her lack of conversation over dinner in the school cafeteria told Goran it was not as easy as she was presenting it.

At night they slept on cots in the classrooms, the desks piled up and pushed to one side. They were divided into separate rooms: adult men, adult women, teenage boys, and teenage girls. Younger children slept with their mothers.

It was cool at night in the classroom but bearably so. There were enough blankets, and the guards and other staff were polite. Goran noticed that the adults spoke in hushed voices. The young people's rooms buzzed with conversation like the dorm rooms at the state-sponsored summer camps he went to every year. Until the talk turned to what they had left behind and what would become of their homes.

The next day it rained. The young men, most of whom had played football outside the day before, were now crowded in the small indoor gymnasium. Goran joined one of the games for a short time, then made an excuse and dropped out when the players on the opposing team started to shove and curse every time they had the ball.

Once outside he found an empty picnic table and pushed it under an awning so that it was mostly shielded from the rain. He sat on top of the table and leaned against the wall of the school. He pressed play on his CD player. He was memorizing the lyrics to every song on U2's *Achtung Baby*.

Goran's eyes were closed when the girl came over to the table. He jumped slightly, embarrassed that he had been mouthing the words.

"Sorry, I didn't mean to startle you. Do you mind if I sit here?"

"No, go ahead."

"I'm tired of being in the room with all those girls. It's either knitting, playing cards, or gossiping about boys they probably won't see for a long time."

"It's basketball for us. One court and, like, eighty guys."

"I'm Nikoleta, from Mostar."

"I'm Goran, from Sarajevo."

"You're Serbian?"

She asked this as nonchalantly as if asking what his favorite color was, or which football team he followed.

"Guilty."

"I'm Muslim. Not that it matters. Or it didn't, before all this."

"Where are you trying to go?"

"Germany. My father has a cousin there. But they don't seem to want to take our papers. You?"

"US. My mother has an aunt there. But now my mom's really tense. I can't tell if it looks good or not."

"What are you listening to?"

"U2."

She smiled. He couldn't tell if the smile meant she thought his choice of music was too obvious, or if she truly liked U2, or if she was just relieved it wasn't one of the local nationalist, turbo-folk bands inciting war. The only thing he knew for sure about her smile is that it hinted at irreverence and self-assurance.

"May I?" she said and reached in the direction of his earphones.

"Here," she continued, moving toward him so she

could put one earpiece next to her ear and he could hold the other next to his.

"Which is your favorite?"

"It's this one," Goran said.

They listened to a few songs this way, their shoulders touching. Goran pressed the pause button when he saw the military vehicles pass on the road outside the school. Three tanks, two personnel carrier trucks filled with young men, some in uniform, some not, and two jeeps pulling cannons that looked to be from World War II creaked by.

Goran reached out to touch Nikoleta's arm and she held on to his. She released it a moment later, then opened her knapsack and pulled out a drawing pad and a charcoal pencil.

"I draw when I get nervous, or anytime really."

"I play guitar. Or I would if I could have brought one with me. That's what I do when I get nervous. Or bored."

He felt her gaze on him as he said this. It was then that Goran noticed her full lips and that Nikoleta was wearing lipstick, or maybe just that her lips were naturally red, and that her green eyes, reddish-brown hair, and pronounced cheekbones all went together.

The rain shifted from a light drizzle to a full-on downpour. Nikoleta put away her drawing pad as the water began to hit it. Even with the awning over them, the rain splashed off the roof and table and onto them. She reached to wipe the drops from Goran's face. He recoiled slightly at the unexpected gesture and immediately wished he hadn't. He knew she could tell how nervous he was.

"You're cute with rain on your face," she said.

"Should we get out of it?" he said.

"I know where," she said.

He nodded.

"Those cars behind the school. No one's ever there and we'll be out of the rain. I'll run first. Wait a minute or two, then come. You know, so no one sees us."

Goran nodded again and she leapt off the table and ran around to the back of the school, out of his view. He waited a minute, put his CD player in his backpack, threw it over his shoulder and ran in the same direction. As he reached the rear of the school, he saw six cars. With the heavy rain he couldn't tell which one she was in. He was getting more soaked with each second he spent outside.

Goran looked in the driver-side door of three of the cars, and then a fourth, and she wasn't in any of them. He wondered for a moment if she had changed her mind and gone inside the school. Looking inside the fifth car, he still couldn't see her. The door opened.

"Get in, quick," she said.

It was a red Yugo with worn, black seats and Nikoleta was sitting in the passenger side in the front. It smelled faintly of gasoline and mildew. They looked at each other and at the steamed-up windows, and laughed.

"We haven't done anything and they're already fogged up," she said.

Goran ran his hands through his hair to rub out the water.

"Play the song again, your favorite one. Translate the words for me."

Goran knew this much: that while he was in the red Yugo with Nikoleta, his mother was inside the school, pleading, explaining, confirming details, desperate to get them out. That nearby, men were amassing weapons. That his relatives waited for word of his family's fate.

That in military barracks, plans were being drawn up for creating enclaves that separated Serbs from Bosniaks from Croatians. That in some camps like these, men and boys were being taken into the woods.

The rain let up slightly as dusk approached. Nikoleta leaned her head on Goran's shoulder as he translated the lyrics for her a third time. She wanted to memorize the song. In a hushed voice, he sang the words to her.

They turned to face each other and he brushed her damp hair away from her face and ran his finger lightly across her lips. Goran wasn't sure about this next part; he had limited experience. He believed the look she gave him was that of a woman asking to be kissed.

◆ ◆ ◆

About a year later, in the afternoon, in their small suburban house in Chicago, Goran found a box in his mother's closet with a collection of her possessions from their previous life. Among them was a VHS tape called *Lepota Poroka—Beauty of Sin*. He recognized the lead actress: Mira Furlan. He remembered his mother speaking of her with admiration. The actress and her husband had left Yugoslavia a year before Goran's family did. Goran recalled his father's words.

Traitors. Too soft to stay and fight for their side. Intellectuals who make noise about what is right and wrong and then leave.

The film, made a few years before the war, tells the story of a couple from rural Montenegro, a place where a woman's infidelity was once punishable by death. A peasant woman—played by Mira Furlan—gets a job as a maid in a nudist holiday resort on the Montenegrin coast.

The images of rural Montenegrin men mistreating women contrasted sharply with the modern, liberal Yugoslavia Goran remembered from his childhood. The scenes of a Western European couple who sexually liberate the beautiful Montenegrin peasant woman were erotic in a casual way that Goran seldomly saw in American films. Early in the film Mira Furlan's character only makes love with her peasant husband while both are fully clothed and her husband covers her head with a black cloth. After her sexual liberation, Mira Furlan's character refuses to have sex with her husband unless she can see and touch his body.

As he watched it, something else about the film caught Goran's attention, a phrase used by the manager of the resort to get her workers to do their jobs. A classic Balkan insult: "You're a goat."

Goran remembered the phrase from his early education in Yugoslav swearing. Such insults were nothing. They were expressions to toss out and laugh about, verbal acrobatics with which to spar. He noticed the difference in the US, which had a much smaller offensive vocabulary. And he learned that in the US such words were much more likely to provoke a fight.

Occasionally, he and his brother Srdjan would trade insults in Serbian, many of which used the phrase *your mother's cunt*. They both understood, as a puppy or a kitten learns the difference between a play bite and a real one, that these were not meant to be taken literally. Until the day that Srdjan brought up Nikoleta.

"Get over her, you goat, there is plenty of *pička* out there."

Goran hated the way this sounded coming from his thirteen-year-old brother.

"How can you still think about that girl? You were a

stupid fourteen-year-old who had barely left your *pička materina*. The smell was probably still on you."

His brother laughed. Goran cursed back at him in their native Serbian.

Fuck you, stupid!

And: *Go to the mountain and fuck goats!*

And: *Sereš na sve strane! You shit in every direction!*

Srdjan laughed again, not taking Goran seriously. Then Goran said, in English: "Fuck off. Just fuck off."

They both knew that when Goran switched to English, he was no longer playing.

The movie also made Goran think of Nikoleta. He imagined that she would grow up to be a woman like Mira Furlan, projecting the unguarded optimism that Goran thought he saw in Mira, a look that said she was open to whatever the world brought. Mira and Nikoleta also had similar reddish hair, green eyes, and movie-worthy cheekbones.

Goran thought about that evening in the red Yugo in the transit camp. He and Nikoleta had kissed for what felt like a long time. He remembered that when they started kissing it was dusk and when he looked up again it was night. In the dim light, Nikoleta unbuttoned her sweater and unhooked her bra and Goran touched her breasts. She undid her jeans and he slid his hand down her underwear. When they heard someone pass nearby, Goran quickly pulled his hands away. As he looked up at her in the faint light, he saw that Nikoleta's eyes were wide open.

Samo za tebe, she said. *Only for you.*

Goran recalled that Nikoleta's skin had felt so soft that it almost startled him, as if his fingers, calloused from his obsessive guitar-playing, might scratch her.

He also remembered the last days at home in Sarajevo

before they had arrived at the transit camp. There had been shouting between his mother and father, more than usual. Objects were thrown. His parents had had one last argument. They made no effort to hide it from Goran and his brother.

You would have us stay and fight? You would risk that?

It's the right side. It's our country too. We can't let them do this.

After all this country has been through, you believe there is a right side?

Go, if that's what you want. I won't stop you.

Will you join us?

I don't know. I have my duty. What if we all left? Who would stay and fight for our side? Would you have us hand our country over to them?

Will you join us?

I don't know, I told you. Do you know how long this war will last? Can you see into the future?

Will you join us?

I don't know.

I need to know.

Will you wait for me if I stay here?

Why won't you promise that you'll join us?

Will you wait for me?

Will you?

I asked you.

...

No.

...

No.

You were just waiting for an excuse.

You were just waiting to give me one.

You fucking goat.

Looking back, Goran realized he couldn't actually remember who called the other a fucking goat or which one accused the other of using the war as an excuse.

In his new bed in his new house in his new country, Goran often fell asleep thinking of the softness of Nikoleta's lips on his cheek, and of her tongue lightly touching his ear as she said, when they finally had to leave the red Yugo: *I won't forget you. I promise. Find me.*

Goran had been raised with enough cynicism to find this trite, and with enough realism to know better. He was moved, but skeptical of the romantic certainty in her voice. He had put his earphones on her and sung one last time.

Love is blindness
I don't want to see
Won't you wrap the night
Around me?
Oh my love
Blindness ...

Goran was crying when his mother showed their papers to the men with guns at the camp gate and they were allowed to leave. Srdjan laughed at him.

"Look, Goran is crying. He met a girl and he had to leave her behind."

They drove through the Serb-controlled region around Banja Luka and into Croatia, and then to Vienna where they sold their car for close to nothing, and then went to the US Embassy and got their papers to travel to the US.

Goran had given Nikoleta his father's address in Sarajevo, and she had given him the address of her grandparents' house in the countryside near Mostar. They knew it was likely a hopeless gesture but it would have felt unbearably sad to part without trying.

◆ ◆ ◆

There was no girl for many years who captivated Goran the way Nikoleta had. He was used to stuffed paprika, *borek* with yoghurt sauce, Turkish coffee, curse-filled conversations with lots of wine, adults who spoke with their hands and with big facial gestures, and going to smoke-filled cafes and outdoor restaurants at the end of the day. His first moment of understanding the mysteries of the female body had been in that red Yugo. How could suburban American girls compare to that?

He met girls in high school, of course. He was cute and articulate enough that they would allow him his few minutes to make his case. Some went out with him; some went out with him a few times. But it was always the girls he had no chance with that he obsessed about.

Girls like Isabella, whom he noticed in his world history class. In a discussion about World War II, he heard her tell a story about her grandfather, who had survived an internment camp for political dissidents in Italy. He thought he saw in Isabella's eyes and felt in her voice that she might understand what the war in Yugoslavia meant.

Plus, he knew Isabella had a boyfriend, an inseparable, permanent boyfriend. The running joke was that they had been dating since pre-school. They stayed in their circle of two most of the time and were so nice, beautiful, and good in all they did that no one seemed to care.

He walked out behind her that day when she mentioned her grandfather's experience in World War II and started a conversation. He guessed he had about three minutes before her boyfriend would appear.

"Do you still have family in Italy? Like, who survived the war? Sounds like it was hard for them."

Isabella looked at Goran as if he were speaking another language.

"I never even knew my grandfather. He died before I was born. My mother just talks about that sometimes and what happened to him."

Goran nodded.

"Yeah, I just ... um," he started. "My family had to leave Yugoslavia because of the war and, so, your grandfather's story made me think about that, you know."

"Oh," she said, pursing her lips as if chewing imaginary bubble gum. She turned away, her eyes scanning the hallway.

Goran imagined dozens of gestures he might have tried and things he might have said. He imagined reaching his arm out to hold hers as he had with Nikoleta. He imagined handing Isabella his earphones to listen to his new favorite R.E.M. song. He imagined mimicking Michael Stipe's dance moves and making Isabella smile. For that one moment his most urgent desire was to know what it would take to make her truly look at him, to whisper something sweet and secretive in his ear.

Isabella smiled the smile that girls learn to extricate themselves from unwanted advances and walked off without saying any more. Goran thought about her for several days, weeks even, discretely watching her, imagining what it might be like to be with her.

◆ ◆ ◆

A few years later, Goran wrote his senior thesis at university on the Yugoslav War. He found articles about the social construction of masculinities in the Balkans and used those to come up with his own reflections on masculinity, xenophobia, and homophobia. He did rudimentary research on Balkan newspaper articles and popular music with nationalistic messages from the time of the war. He graduated with honors and his advisor suggested he continue this research in graduate school.

With a scholarship letter confirming funds for his doctorate, he decided to use his savings to travel to Bosnia to see his father. The war was over, and although ethnic tensions were alive and well, it was safe to travel there. He called his mother to get information on how to contact his father.

"I think he's still in Sarajevo, last I heard of him. Still in the military, or maybe working with the government, I think. Are you sure you want to go ..."

"I thought he fought with the Serbs. I thought he would be in Serbia or at least in the Republika Srpska."

His mother was silent, then responded.

"No, he stayed in Sarajevo."

"My father's a Serb from Sarajevo who fought on the side of the Bosnian armed forces against the Serbs in the war?"

"You remember that he worked in the education ministry before the war? Then he was drafted by the Serbian Army when the war started, back when it was still called the Yugoslavian Army."

"Yeah, I know that part."

"He joined the Bosnian side. He thought it was the right thing to do. That he was from Sarajevo and should stay and fight for Sarajevo."

"Why didn't you ever tell me that?"

"What difference does it make?"

"Because he wasn't on the side that was carrying out mass rape and slaughtering civilians. He didn't buy into the ethnic bullshit that fueled the war."

"Do you think they were growing flowers and raising baby rabbits on the Bosniak side?" she said.

"You know it's not the same."

"When you have two teenage sons who you want to keep safe, it's the same. If we had stayed, assuming we made it through the siege of Sarajevo, you would have been drafted. Do you think I cared which side your father was on? Have you ever stopped to think about why I did that? Bring you and Srdjan to the US?"

Goran was silent on the other end of the phone. He rarely spoke back to her because he knew she would throw this question at him.

"It matters to *me* which side he was on. Of course it matters which side he was on. You should have told me," he stammered.

"You never asked."

"I just thought ..."

He stopped. The words passed through Goran's head but he didn't say them. *You're both fucking goats. You and my father.*

"Goran ..."

He hung up.

MUSEUM SUBMISSION 7-2009

A lot of my friends on the island, professional women like me, have taken to working class men. There is no shame in it.

Mine was a solid man. Caring. Finished his secondary school.

There are benefits to having a man who knows how to fix a car or your sink and will carry that heavy suitcase you bring back with all the things you buy on your trip to New York or Toronto.

We were together for nearly four years. There were moments when we ran out of things to talk about. But most of the time it was good.

He worked for a construction firm. They build resorts and repair them and clean up after the hurricanes.

One night after a couple of glasses of rum he told me that when he was seventeen he had sex with a white woman for money, at one of the resorts in Ocho Rios. He had been working there on a construction site. One of his workmates had told him that he sometimes slept with white women to make a little extra money. And for the fun of it. So my husband had thought, why not?

I couldn't get that image out of my head. I wanted to ask a hundred questions. Did he enjoy it? Was she attractive to him? Was it hard to get excited? Did she ask him for it more than once?

I don't remember how long afterwards it was when I had a colleague visiting from abroad. I invited her to our house for dinner along with a group of my work colleagues.

My husband was serving drinks, and helping our housekeeper cook. All the women complemented him on his rum punch and on the jerk chicken he had made. I knew none of them had husbands who cooked for them.

I laughed and told the women to keep their hands off of him. He's not for sale. Not like those boys at the resorts, I said.

All the women laughed. My husband did not.

I thought about the words as I said them. I had that slow motion feeling of having said something that was off. But with the rum in my head it just came out. I thought about how I might apologize later.

My husband excused himself after dinner. I thought he would return to say goodbye to our guests but he didn't.

It was only after all the guests had left and I helped our housekeeper finish cleaning up that I realized he had gone out. He didn't come back that night and he didn't answer his mobile phone. I tried to fall asleep by convincing myself that he was angry but that he would come back, and that he would accept my apology.

The next morning I called his sister. She told me he had called her that morning and told her he was going somewhere in the Caribbean but he wouldn't tell her where.

When I got home from work that night, I went to his study. Under one of his books I found the note.

You're right. I'm not for sale, it said.

I made myself a second drink to try to sleep. But before I did, I looked at our bank account. He had transferred all of our savings to a bank in Grand Cayman.

I laughed for a few days when I told this to my friends. Until I started to cry.

These are the work gloves from when he was a foreman building resorts. And this is the massage oil he used on me after he took off the gloves and after he showered from his daily work in the hot island sun. After he came to me. Before he told me about the white woman at the beach and before I said that horrible thing.

Kingston, Jamaica, 2009

Katia

Goran and Katia sat on the floor leaning against the couch in his apartment. It was their fourth evening together as a couple. A nearly empty bottle of red wine stood next to Goran. He asked Katia why she wanted to be a therapist.

"I'm not always entirely sure, to be honest. Curiosity, I think, about how our childhood affects us. Then some days I think it's because my parents made *me* go to a therapist. Even though it should have been them telling me about my birth mother and how I was adopted and everything that happened when they lived in Brazil. It's weird, but it's like I felt part of the time that my therapist was totally incompetent. And then when I stopped being mad at her, I felt this deep empathy toward her. You know, for how hard she was trying to help me make sense out of it all. When really we didn't have much to go on."

"What did your parents tell you?"

"Only that they adopted me when they lived in Rio de Janeiro for a few years for their work. That my biological mother was a teenager, from a *favela*, and that she died not long after I was born."

"What was that like?"

"I don't know. It's not like I have another childhood to compare mine to. They're my parents and I'm their daughter. I don't look like them, of course, which is kind of weird, I guess. They had a son before me, a biological son. I would have had an older brother. He died in an accident in Brazil."

"That's a lot for parents to live with."

"Yeah, I know."

"That explains the look in their eyes. From when you showed me their picture."

"What do you mean?"

"They look sad, like they've lost something."

"I guess I never even saw that. That's just their normal look to me."

She paused.

"The hardest part is just how little they told me."

He nodded: "I wasn't adopted but sometimes I have the same feeling. Like, even though my parents are my biological parents, I don't know who they really are. With my mom, it's almost like surgery to extract some parts of the past from her, about her life in Yugoslavia. Let alone about my father, who I've met only once since we left Sarajevo and is now a complete stranger to me."

"I asked my parents about my brother, their son, about what he was like and how it happened that he was run over by a motorcycle. I was maybe twelve. We were watching a show on television, one of those rescue-the-Amazon stories with reporters going in boats up the river to see where the trees are being cut down. So I asked Kevin about my brother, about the accident. He got this look. It looked like he was holding his breath and he closed his eyes for a second like he was trying to control his tears. 'Someday I'll tell you.' That's all he would say."

"Why do you call him Kevin?"

"He's just Kevin."

"Not father or Dad?"

"No."

"Never Daddy?"

"Nope, not for as long as I can remember."

"And your mother? Do you call her Mom?"

"Yeah, of course."

Goran gave the slightest grin.

"What do you think it would have been like if your brother had lived? The adopted daughter and the biological son?"

"No idea. There were so many other things in my head then. What would it have been like if I had red hair and white skin and freckles like my mother? If it hadn't been obvious every moment I was next to her or Kevin that I was adopted?"

"Did you ever think of going to Brazil? I mean, to find your biological family."

"Maybe I will someday. Sometimes I think I know as much as I want to. I don't know about your parents, but mine couldn't talk to me about sex. The way they told me was they just left those books out, *Joy of Sex* and *A Doctor Talks to 13-Year-Olds About Sex* and stuff like that. It was kind of the same when I read about my biological mother."

"How so?"

"They showed me a copy of a newspaper article. I only know a few phrases and words in Portuguese, so it took me a while to understand it all. But I recognized the name, my biological mother's name. And then I understood the word *morta*. Dead. When I saw it there, in print, suddenly it felt real, I guess."

Goran reached out to touch her arm.

"I hated them for a couple of days and then I calmed myself down enough to make them tell me. At first I wanted to yell at them. Like tell me the fucking truth. The article said she was caught up in drug violence. And then I understood why they hadn't told me before."

He looked at her, waiting.

"We don't let little girls grow up knowing that their mother was killed in a gang war. Right?"

He nodded and said nothing more, reaching his arm around her. She couldn't say that she loved him right then; it was far too soon. But after that night, she judged him worthy of love.

◆ ◆ ◆

He did not take her hand when she reached out to take his as they left the museum in Zagreb that day.

"Do you want to talk about her? About what happened in the camp and afterward?"

He gave her a cold glare.

"Please, Katia, don't try to be my therapist."

"I'm not. We're living together. I'm your girlfriend, or partner, or whatever we call ourselves, and I'm trying to be supportive."

"Yeah, well, support won't really go back and fix what happened in the war. You know? Some things can't be fixed just by talking about them."

"I know that. But I'd like to understand."

"Stop it, would you? Stop sounding like a ... like a therapist."

She could tell that he had worked hard to keep from saying *fucking* therapist.

Katia knew it was not about her, that the letter in the museum had taken Goran to a place he had avoided for years. She knew the stories, of course, the reports of women and girls held in sexual slavery, the ethnic cleansing, the massacre of Bosnian men and boys by Serbian paramilitary groups. But it had all been just that, stories. Things happening far away. Goran had shared with her pieces of his past, the father left behind, his mother's new husband, life as an immigrant. But he had never mentioned the girl in the transit camp.

After a few minutes of walking in silence, he switched on his tour-guide mode again and began narrating the old town of Zagreb for her as if nothing had happened. As if they hadn't just stumbled onto his past in the museum. As if he hadn't stood before that CD and that drawing and cried.

◆ ◆ ◆

Two days later they rented a car and drove the four hours from Zagreb to the Croatian coast. He had chosen a medieval beach town with cobblestone streets and a small, pebbly beach. There were some Russian and German tourists, but mostly it was empty, still a couple of months before the summer season. It was just warm enough to be outside in their swimsuits in the middle of the day but the water was too cold to get in.

She had felt his eyes on her when she had her bikini on earlier at the beach in a way that made her feel desired and safe.

Later that night, lying on her back in the darkness, she returned to the topic.

"Did you get an address?"

"What?"

"So you can find her?"

He was silent.

"Katia, please, just leave it."

"You should find her, Goran."

"Katia, can we think about something else? Is this what you're thinking about? We're here. We have …"

"It was a powerful letter," she said, cutting him off.

"She's obviously thought a lot about it. About you. You were crying, which is not something I've ever seen you do before. I was moved by it too. I'm sure everyone at the museum who reads it is too. It's a beautiful story. It's amazing that you found it."

"Katia, I'm here with you. I don't want to think about that now."

"But you're not here. That's the point."

He turned his back to her.

She stared at the ceiling. She could hear the gentle lapping of the sea in the distance. She moved toward him, putting her face against his upper back, and smelled him. At least this part was the same. She listened to his breathing mixed with the faint sound of the sea. With each small wave she heard, he seemed to be drifting farther away from her. She told herself not to panic.

MUSEUM SUBMISSION 97-2012

I moved to Galveston to take a job as a surgical nurse. At first I was worried about how it might be for me, as a lesbian in Texas, but that wasn't a big deal in the end. I was there for barely three weeks when I met a doctor and fell in love.

See, if you want to smoke and you work at the hospital, you have to do it far away. One night, I saw this doctor staring at me while I was standing outside the parking lot, smoking. It was one of those outrageously hot and humid Galveston nights. She asked if she could have one.

I remember what she said: If you work here, you have to really want to smoke, right?

Sublimation, I answered.

She laughed.

From that night on, between our shifts, we went back and

forth from her place to mine. We didn't want to think about how work might play into it all.

It was the first time I had worked in intensive care. Right off the bat I had a man with a heart transplant that didn't take. We had to keep him open for part of the time, trying to get his body to accept it and keeping him on the heart pump. First he lost a leg. We had to amputate just above the knee. Then he started to lose feeling in his arms.

The guy was young and seemed really nice but the only person who came to visit him was his older brother. We're not supposed to eavesdrop. But it sounded like deep family shit, divorce and step-parents and arguments about inheritance.

The guy was ready to die. Late at night he would tell me that he couldn't take it any more. That he had made peace with it. But his brother wanted him to keep trying. The brother was a real pain in the ass, yelling at us nurses and at his younger brother for giving up.

My girlfriend was the lead cardiologist on his case. She wouldn't acknowledge that it was going south for the guy. I told her we had to let him go. Then she went into this whole macho thing like failure is not an option. And she told me I was just a nurse on the case and I should focus on my job. Leave the decisions to the doctors. And then I told her she was just like the asshole men doctors who think they're God and don't know when to give up.

The older brother wasn't even there in the end. And neither was my girlfriend. I held the guy's hand when we finally turned off the machines.

My girlfriend and I never said another word to each other.

I rehearsed a dozen ways to say I was sorry. And I imagined as many ways that she would come up to me on my break and apologize. For months I fantasized about us getting back together.

About six months later I heard that she moved to take a position at the medical center in Houston. I stopped smoking that same week.

This is the last box of cigarettes I ever smoked. And this is the T-shirt the guy came in with. A Nick Cave concert T-shirt. His brother told me to throw it away.

I don't even know why I kept these two things. I wanted to get rid of them. But I wanted to send them somewhere where I could find them if I needed to be reminded. It's good to be reminded.

Galveston, USA, 2012

Tyler

The apartment complex was a non-descript, two-story, 1970s highway motel-style building with ten units on each floor, black metal stairs connecting the two levels. Anyone driving by would not have given it a second look. Unless they knew that it was a shelter for abused women.

Tyler saw the women's closed blinds, the pizza boxes in the trash, and the plastic garbage bags filled with disposable diapers and milk cartons. When he encountered the women he either looked away or tipped his hat and made brief eye contact. He knew he was given free rent to keep a watch out for ex-husbands and ex-boyfriends. *Make them feel safe. Keep them safe. But keep your distance.* After Sammy came to live with him, Tyler was even more diligent about not talking to them.

Sammy was looking again at the Big Wheel outside the apartment a few doors down. He tentatively approached it as if it called out to him.

The door opened and the owner of the Big Wheel came outside.

"Sammy, that's not yours," Tyler said.

The dark-haired, dark-eyed woman spoke before her son could.

"That's okay. Is that okay, Joaquin? Can he ride it?"

"Do you know how?" the boy said to Sammy. He had an authoritative voice for such a small boy.

Sammy shrugged.

"I'll show you," Joaquin said.

"They can't help it," the woman said to Tyler. "The desire to ride is more powerful than they are."

"Tell me about it," Tyler said, nodding at his own motorcycle that had remained under its cover ever since Sammy had moved in.

He hesitated before moving in her direction.

"Hey, I'm Tyler," he said

"Yeah, I know. You're our cop. I'm Carla."

"Sorry, I guess I should have introduced myself before. Kind of not supposed to be social, you know, just be around."

"It's okay."

"Well, good to meet you. We're going to his grandmother's in Houston, so we should get on the road," Tyler said.

"Send him over to play sometime if you want. Joaquin misses his neighbor friends since we … moved here."

Tyler looked at her as if she had just invited him to vandalize a car.

"It's okay. Really," Carla said.

He smiled at her and for the first time he let his eyes fully meet hers.

◆ ◆ ◆

Gradually, Tyler let Sammy outside the apartment more to play with Joaquin. He watched as the two boys interacted. Tyler stayed outside his door, leaning on the railing, and when Carla stepped out of her apartment, they nodded to confirm that the boys were safe.

One Saturday Tyler took both Sammy and Joaquin for a hike at a nature reserve nearby. He sprayed the boys with bug repellent and they scrunched their noses at the smell of it. He imitated them and they laughed. They were away for nearly two hours, walking on the trails of pine and live oaks that led to the Colorado River and then back to the main visitors center.

Both of the boys were asleep for most of the drive back; it was the first quiet moment on the outing. As Tyler activated the remote control that opened the gate to the apartment complex and pulled his car into the parking lot, the two boys woke up.

"I'm hungry," Joaquin said.

"Me too."

"Pizza!"

"Pizza! Pizza!" the two boys said in unison both giggling.

Tyler turned and looked back at them.

"Well, you'll have to ask your mother."

Joaquin stepped out the car, then stopped.

"Can my Mom come too?"

"Of course."

A few minutes later, Carla appeared at the driver's side of the car.

"Hey. Thanks for taking him on the hike. My sister is coming over for dinner but thanks for the offer. Another time?"

"Sure," he said.

The next day, Tyler had another session with his therapist. He stared at his phone while he waited for her to finish something on her laptop. Tyler glanced at her when she wasn't looking. He tried to understand her posture, why it was she held her legs as if she was about to jump at a moment's notice. He noted too that her sleeveless dress showed off her pronounced collar bones and her cinnamon-colored arms.

"So, Tyler, let's talk about how it was coming back from Afghanistan."

He looked to the floor, then up and to the side, and out the window.

"I think the worst part was about two months after I came home."

"How so?"

"Because of my friend Cole. My last tour of duty overlapped partly with his. He was one of my best friends in high school. He came home from Afghanistan a few months before me. And I tried to call him, you know, but he just ignored my calls. And then I was getting my life back together here. I got the patrol job in Bastrop and then I moved into the women's shelter and I just stopped trying to call him after a while. The days were nonstop and ..."

He stopped again, this time longer.

"What happened?"

Tyler looked away from her. He rubbed the stubble on his face and clasped his hands over his lips.

"He killed himself. Gun to his head. Sitting in his car late at night on the side of the road near where I-10 hits 71. His mom called to tell me when they found him the next day. There was so much pain in her voice that it hurt just to hear her breathe. She asked me to be a pallbearer and if I wanted to say some words at the funeral.

"So afterwards we were at his parents' house. And his mom was crying and all and she asked me how is it that they can protect us from bullets and bombs but not from the demons we bring back home. I didn't know what to tell her. What was I going to say? That I probably knew more soldiers who thought about killing themselves than were killed by the Taliban? That we're probably better at killing ourselves than the Taliban are at killing us?"

"And what do you think about Cole killing himself?"

"I don't."

"What do you mean?"

"That I don't think about it. I mean I do my best not to think about it. I have Sammy and these women who need me. That's what I need to think about. What I try to think about anyway."

"But you do think about it?"

"Everybody who's been there thinks about what we had to do. And what we saw. You can't stop thinking about it. And then there's that fear, you know. It gets into you. I mean, the Taliban weren't very good at killing us when it comes right down to it; I mean in the classic way we fight wars. But they sure as hell know how to scare the shit out of us. You can't take a step, drive a single click, look at a single Afghan without thinking about when the next explosion will come. Or the next car bomb or the next ambush. The next IED. Thinking that any man you see, and maybe even the women and children, might have a gun or a grenade or a bomb strapped on. You don't just turn that off when you come home. They don't want us to talk about that part."

"Who is *they*?"

"The people who sent us over there. They don't want us to talk about how scared and how messed up we are from walking around like that for months and years at a time. Wouldn't it be great if they could admit that part? That we're losing in Afghanistan and we'll always lose because the Taliban know how to scare the shit out of us and that it eats us up from the inside."

"How do you deal with that?"

"I'm just thankful every day that I have Sammy. I don't know how I would be if I didn't have him. I don't know why Melissa left him with me and I don't know where she is. Maybe I should want to know and maybe I should try to find her. But I'm happy she did it."

"Let's go back to your friend Cole for a minute."

Tyler looked up at the clock: three minutes left in the session.

"How about we talk about him next time? I have to go pick up my boy."

◆ ◆ ◆

A few days later, after he came off patrol and the babysitter had left, there was a knock at the door. It was Carla.

"Hey, I know it's a school night, but you two want to go get a pizza with us?"

Tyler scratched his head, looking down to the ground. Before he could say anything, Sammy came running into the room.

"Yeah, come on, daddy."

It was the first time Sammy had used this word. He looked at Sammy, then finally spoke.

"Yeah, sure," he said. Then, turning to Carla, he continued: "Give us a few."

Carla nodded and, reaching for Joaquin's hand, stepped out of the apartment while Tyler and Sammy got ready.

After pizza there was ice cream. The boys' usual bedtime had come and gone by the time they drove back. Both of the boys slept in the backseat again.

"Hey, I'll carry Joaquin upstairs for you before I take Sammy to bed," Tyler said as they pulled into the parking lot.

"Thanks," Carla said, opening the doors for him.

Tyler tried not to get comfortable in Carla's apartment. He walked with a police officer's efficiency and discretion, moving to put Joaquin gently on his bed and leaving the boy's bedroom just as quickly as he entered.

"Tyler, do you want to bring Sammy in here for a few minutes and I'll make some coffee, or we can have a glass of wine?" she asked.

He stopped at the door and looked back at her. Her eyes caught his; he knew she could read his hesitation.

"I'm sure the crisis center allows you to have coffee with us."

He smiled and scratched the back of his head.

"Yeah, just for a little bit, I suppose. I'll get Sammy."

"You can put him on the couch in Joaquin's room."

Tyler accepted a beer and Carla poured herself a glass of wine. He sat on the edge of her couch.

"Where's Sammy's mother? I mean, if you don't mind me asking."

"Honest truth? I don't know. I was in Afghanistan. Joined up, like lots of guys do. I had just broken up with Sammy's mother. And I thought joining up was the thing to do. My dad had served way back when and it seemed like a good time for me to, you know, do my part. Thing is, I didn't even know Melissa was pregnant. She didn't tell me about Sammy until I came back from my last tour of duty and Sammy was already four. That was a few months ago."

"She left him with you, just like that?"

"Yeah, she called out of the blue, just brought him over and left him. Sent me his birth certificate, gave me sole custody. Then disappeared."

"Have you tried to find her?"

He raised an eyebrow.

"Figure she doesn't want to be a mother. I have no idea why. It's been so crazy just keeping up with Sammy that I guess I haven't had time to think about it much. I mean, I could probably find her if I really wanted to, but I figure

I can't make her be a mother. I called a friend of hers who told me that Melissa planned this for a while. That's all I know."

"You seem to be doing alright as a father."

"I'm trying."

"How did things go for you in Afghanistan? Sorry, I know that's not exactly a light conversation."

"No, it's okay. I think I had it pretty easy compared to a lot of guys."

He was glad Carla could tell he didn't want to say much more about his time in the military, and that she did not insist.

"My ex was in Afghanistan. It messed him up. It's not like he was a soft and easy guy before he joined, but when he came back he had this edge to him. He knew it, too. I think he really tried to do right by us. I really do. I think he used all his energy to try to be the father and husband he knew he should be. He made it his mission after he came back. But he couldn't. I don't even recognize the man the military sent back to me."

Tyler nodded.

"I think part of the reason he's so angry now is that he lost control. Instead of feeling sorry for what he did, he feels angry at himself that he lost control. And now he's turned into this man I don't even know anymore. When the cops came I thought they might have to use a Taser on him. And I wouldn't have blamed them."

Tyler looked at her longer this time before turning away.

"It's been really hard for Joaquin. He saw it all. It's hard to explain to a boy that his father has turned into this violent man who can't see us anymore because he might hurt us again."

Carla looked up and met his eyes. Tyler wondered

whether the hairs on her arm had stood on end like his did when they had brushed against each other. He knew he shouldn't be here, and that he shouldn't be thinking this.

MUSEUM SUBMISSION 17-2011

I was his third wife. He told me he wanted me to give him a son. I am sure he suspected I was using birth control.

I didn't tell him that I had applied for a scholarship to come to France. I was the only one of his wives who had studied beyond primary school. I was a schoolteacher. He made me stop teaching when we got married.

The women here, the French women, they don't understand how we live. It's not so bad having the other wives, I tell them. You have help and you have friends. And he comes around for you every few nights, not every night. I was glad for that.

I tell the French women that I feel sorry for them. They look at me like I'm crazy. I tell them that they look lonely in their apartments with only two or three people. It is so quiet in their houses. With three wives and seven children we were never lonely.

He was usually quiet the nights he came to my room. Sometimes he talked about money and corruption, about how his brothers or some government officials were always trying to take his money from him and how he could never get ahead. The usual things men talk about.

I swore to him that I would come back after the scholarship. I swore to him and to my family and to the international agency that paid for the scholarship and to the French government. But I am here.

This is the Quran his family gave me the day we were married. They knew I could read. I knew which parts of the Quran they wanted me to read.

I think that if he had only married one woman, I would be the one he would have chosen. I wonder if he has already taken another wife. Whether I have been replaced. The French women can't understand how I could love a man like him. With many wives.

Marseille, France, 2011

Goran

After that argument with his mother, when he wanted to call her a fucking goat, he was even more convinced that he needed to go to Sarajevo to find his father.

It was the summer before Goran started his doctorate. He had no hotel reservation, nor had he made contact with relatives who still lived in Sarajevo. From the information desk at the airport he chose a simple hotel in the city center, caught the bus into town, dropped his bag in his room, and set out walking.

The handful of buildings still in ruin and the pockmarks from shellings were the only overt signs of the war. But they were enough to make it seem like a battered and bruised version of his childhood Sarajevo. He felt a mild disdain at this, that the city had not been restored to its pre-war state. He knew that was an American's way of thinking as soon as he thought it.

Goran followed the route his father used to take on evening strolls, starting at the newest part of the city with its utilitarian, socialist modern architecture, into the Austro-Hungarian section, and ending in the old part of the city, built under Ottoman rule.

The north wind brought scattered rain and cool air from the mountains. Although his thoughts came to him in English now, words from his childhood language crawled out from hidden corners of his brain. He stepped into a coffee shop and squinted as he felt the pungent cigarette smoke hit his nose and eyes.

As Goran ordered a Turkish coffee and a *burek*, the Serbian words felt strange in his mouth. The last time he had been in Sarajevo, Serbian families were being airlifted from Bosnia to Serbia and his family was busy packing things and abandoning his childhood home. Goran remembered his parents arguing about whether they would lose their house if they fled and where they would live when they came back.

Goran knew he could be here, drink coffee, walk these streets and seem like a local. Yet he couldn't shake the feeling that they could tell that he was one of those who made it out before the siege, and that, even if his father had fought on the Bosnian side, Goran was still Serbian. He had to remind himself that he didn't have *Serb* tattooed on his forehead.

A dozen times that first day back in Sarajevo he imagined he had seen Nikoleta passing in the distance. She would be slightly taller, wearing tight jeans like the other girls on the streets, her reddish hair pulled back, thick, dark eyeliner accentuating her assured and irreverent gaze. He imagined she would have moved here for her university studies, and that she would have wanted to be away from her family's tight control.

Goran envisioned her stopping on the street, recognizing him, looking up from under an umbrella or a hooded rain jacket. They would step into a café and then they would resume whatever it was they had started in that parked car in the transit camp. He spent a long time imagining the sex. But it was more than that.

In this imaginary reunion, Goran skipped the exact moment when they looked at each other and made eye contact and visualizing whether they would embrace, or kiss, or what they would say at that first moment of reencounter. Instead, he'd jump to the moment after that. The moment when they were back together as they always should have been, the awkward silences miraculously filled and the time between the transit camp and finding each other again rendered meaningless.

He left the coffee shop and continued wandering down the narrow, pedestrian streets of the old town. He came across a bookstore with English, German, and Serbo-Bosnian books. A clerk dressed mostly in grey and black, with a slight stoop, who seemed to be in his forties, smiled at him.

"Anything you're looking for?" the man said in Bosnian.

"No, just browsing."

The man looked at him, with a friendly but scrutinizing face.

"Are you from here?"

"My family left in '92. I live in the US now."

"Don't tell me. Chicago?"

"Yes."

"First time back?"

"Yeah."

Goran looked at the man, and guessed that he was trying to place Goran—Serbian, or Bosnian, or something else.

"It must be strange, being back for the first time. You would have been a teenager back then."

Goran nodded.

"Do you wonder if we hate you? For leaving, I mean, while we lived through the siege, or maybe because you're a Serb?"

Goran looked on.

"What's your name?"

"Goran."

"A good Serbian name. So, do you? Do you wonder if

we hate you for being Serbian and for leaving?"

The man smiled as he asked this question, so Goran awkwardly smiled back. Before he answered, the man continued.

"Just in case I'm the first one to say it, welcome back. I don't know what your family told you, but if we hate you, it's because you were lucky enough to get out. Not for being Serbian. *Pička*, we had Muslims siding with the Serbs. We had Serbs siding with us, and Serbs who were our neighbors who became our enemies. We have a long list of people to hate. But you're too young to have been part of that."

He asked Goran what he studied and where. When Goran mentioned his work on masculinities, the man pointed him to some books he thought Goran might find interesting.

"I'm Muslim, *Bosniak*," the man continued. "My wife is Serbian like you. Orthodox. You know, prays to Jesus. I grew up going to the Islamic school right down the street there, across from the mosque where my family still prays. I dropped out and went to public school. If you ask me, the way her family talks about Jesus, and they way mine talks about the Prophet, peace be upon him, it's all the same thing. They talk about them both like they're mascots for some kind of holy battle.

"My family cut me off when I started seeing her. My mother couldn't take it. Wouldn't talk to me for years. It was nearly ten years later, after our son was born, before my mother would talk to my wife."

Goran looked at him. The man paused.

"Some here may hate you. But they've been hating members of their own families for a long time already. So, if they hate you, my friend, don't take it personally. We all hold grudges here."

Goran continued browsing, purchased two books and started to leave.

"Come back again," the man said. "When you write your book on our stupid men and how we raise our boys to be thugs, show it to us."

Back in his hotel room Goran stared at the pages of the books he had bought and tried to concentrate, to make the Serbian words come back to him. But he was distracted. He had been putting off what he had come for.

He stared at the phone in the hotel room. Then he ran his hand over the receiver. Goran read and re-read the instruction sheet on how to make local calls. He looked out the window onto the grey, rain-covered streets and then back at the phone.

Night had fallen by the time Goran dialed the number.

"*Zdravo*," a man's voice answered in Serbian. Goran recognized the voice.

Goran fell silent; the voice caught him off guard.

"Hello?" the man said again, in Serbian. "What do you want?"

"*To je Goran. Ja sam ovde u Sarajevu*," he said.

Now it was his father's turn to be silent. Goran heard his father yell something away from the phone and then he spoke again.

"Okay. Okay. Hello, Goran," his father responded. "You want something, maybe? Shall we meet?"

"Just to meet," Goran said.

He thought his father sounded caught off guard and slightly annoyed. As if Goran had violated some unspoken agreement or secret treaty. As if his father might say next: *Didn't you know you were never supposed to call me here?*

◆ ◆ ◆

The meeting was at his father's office in the city government building with its imposing Ottoman-style architecture. As Goran entered the building, he asked the guard where to find the city planning department and said his father's name.

The building smelled of thick layers of cigarette smoke, despite the no-smoking signs in every hallway. Goran stopped at the doorway to the office. His father was staring at his computer screen. He looked up as Goran walked in, and stood up to shake Goran's hand. He did not smile.

Goran felt his heart race. His father motioned for Goran to sit down in one of the chairs in front of his desk and Goran did so. He looked at the pictures on the wall and on the desk. He recognized some of the men in the pictures with his father. There was one picture of his father with Rasim Delić, head of the Bosnian army for most of the war, and another picture of his father with US General Wesley Clark. And there was a picture of his father and a woman along with a girl and a boy, both teenagers. He guessed this was his father's new family. There were no pictures of him or of his brother, Srdjan.

"So Goran, here you are, all grown up," his father said.

Goran looked at his father.

"Did your mother suggest that you come find me?"

His tone was nonchalant, as if he were asking how Goran's flight had been.

"No, she was against the idea. She thought it might be dangerous for me in Sarajevo."

His father chuckled.

"Dangerous for you to know more about where you're from? Or does she think they attack Serbs here?" his father said.

"It was my idea to come. I wanted to see you."

"So, you must be in university, no? How old are you, twenty-two, twenty-three? What do you study?"

"Sociology. Gender studies. I write about identity and masculinities. I just started my doctorate."

"I see," his father said, nodding. Goran thought he could see disappointment. "You must have much to say about us."

His father had said *us* as if separating Goran from him and all the other real Balkan men.

"Yes, about *us*," Goran said.

"And Srdjan, what's he up to?"

"He's well. Studying civil engineering. Wants to build things. Seems the same as he was when he was twelve. Just bigger."

His father smiled.

"Engineering, that's a good profession."

Silence settled in the space between them.

"So, life is good for you in America."

Goran wanted to think that was a question. Before he could answer, his father opened his desk drawer, pulled out a bottle, opened it and took out two small glasses.

"*Rakija?*"

Goran accepted. He took a sip without toasting his father. It burned in his mouth and then, slowly, it calmed him.

"I didn't know all this time that you sided with the Bosniaks, that you stayed in Sarajevo and fought on their side. My mother, I mean Mom, never told me anything about it until I told her I was coming here."

His father nodded and sipped his rakija.

"No, I guess she wouldn't tell you. That wasn't something that mattered to her. She wanted to get out of here. To go to America. She had always wanted that. Long before the war."

"She wanted to protect us."

"Yes, so she said."

"How was it? I mean, during the siege and all?"

His father poured Goran another shot of rakija.

"You can get used to hell. And we've had a lot of experience. You surprise yourself by how quickly you can get used to things. But, as you probably know, it was hell for your mother and me even before the war."

Goran looked at his father and felt the rakija warm him.

"Some people wanted to make us into heroes, us Serbs fighting on the Bosniak side. As if every third Serb in Sarajevo isn't married to a Croat or Bosniak or hasn't fucked one at some time or another. Some of us were avoiding arrest and choosing to side with the Bosniaks and some of us were following our hearts and doing what we thought was right. I could never think of myself as anything but a Yugoslavian from Bosnia. Why would I not fight on the side of those from the same town as me? On the side of my neighbors? The guys I went to school with? The families of the girls I had been with? I don't see what is heroic about that."

His father turned to look out the window for a moment as if the memories were there, outside.

"So what was it like? Were we Serbs who stayed here heroes saving the downtrodden Bosniaks from the evil Chetniks? That's what the journalists always want to know when they come from Europe or America to interview us.

"Do you remember that very nice man who lived next door to us? He had that beautiful shaggy dog. It would always come into our yard and sometimes tear down our laundry. You and Srdjan loved the dog so much that we could never get very upset about it. Maybe you remember the man. Lazar. His wife would bring us pears from their tree in the summer and he would give us a bottle of plum rakija during the holidays."

Goran nodded, feeling that this was how they could be, a father reminiscing to his son, in the language they both grew up in.

"He was a Serb nationalist. All their Chetnik bullshit about a Greater Serbia. Going back to whatever ancient history from the fourteenth century or whatever the fuck ignorance they use to justify why they hated Muslims and why the Muslims were to blame for everything that led Yugoslavia to fall apart. He stayed at the beginning of the war, stayed in Sarajevo. Sent his family to Belgrade but he stayed behind. I think he was afraid they would lose their house. Lots of us were."

His father put down his glass, took out a cigarette, lit it, and then took another drink.

"I don't know what to think about him. Misguided. He heard all that Serbian nationalist bullshit and believed it. Maybe he gave money to support the militias. Maybe he hid Chetnik snipers in his house. I don't know. He wasn't dangerous, I don't think. Stupid and racist. But not dangerous."

His father shook his head and looked out the window before he continued.

"I was sent to find him. That would prove to the Bosniaks that I was really on their side."

His father exhaled loudly, then looked back at Goran.

"That fucking sweet dog was there. The dog was looking up at me. I think he recognized me, you know, just staring at me, wagging his tail. He jumped up at me, licking me."

As his father said this, Goran remembered the dog. He could picture it. He thought he could remember its smell.

"I killed the dog first."

His father stopped and rested his hand on his glass, running his finger around the brim.

"So, sure, I was one of the good guys. Don't you think?"

His father held up his glass of rakija as if toasting the air, when the phone rang.

"Yes, my love. Of course," his father said into the receiver.

He looked back at Goran.

"I must go. There is a reception at my son's school. He is studying to be an architect. His second year. And then I have to take him to mosque. Not my idea, of course. My wife is Muslim. He goes for her sake."

Goran waited for something, for a suggestion of another meeting, or an invitation to dinner to meet this other family and his half-brother and half-sister.

"Good luck, Goran. It was good to see you. Give my regards to Srdjan."

His father reached out his glass and Goran corresponded out of politeness.

"Živeli," he said.

"Živeli."

Goran waited, thinking there would be more. There had to be more. He believed that his father, with some dramatic aplomb, would say more, or at the very least send more words, something more, to his mother or his brother. He remembered moments from his childhood of his father and uncles and cousins drinking rakija or wine together and laughing loudly, hugging each other affectionately, sometimes crying in loud, slurred voices, telling grandiose truths or even more grandiose lies.

His father stood up, put a newspaper and a pack of cigarettes into the pocket of his overcoat, and stood at the door waiting for Goran. He followed his father down the flights of stairs to the main entrance.

"My car is out the back, so I will leave you here. I hope you enjoy Sarajevo. It's good you came to see it again."

His father shook Goran's hand and walked away. Goran stared after him, but his father did not turn around.

◆ ◆ ◆

The next morning Goran went back to the bookstore. The man smiled when he saw him.

"It's the prodigal Serb. Any luck finding your family?"

"My father."

"He moved back after the war?"

"Stayed. He fought on the Bosnian side."

"Oh yeah? We have a few of those. Considered traitors by most Serbs and never really trusted by Bosnians. Either really brave or really stubborn. You haven't seen him all these years?"

"No. My mother remarried in America and he never contacted us. I just found out my father married a Muslim woman after we left."

"Maybe he knew this woman before the war. Don't be offended, these things happen all the time here. Forbidden love. The most interesting kind. I can tell you."

Goran looked at the man. With all this new information at once, he hadn't thought about it before. If his father's new son was in his second year of university, he would be the same age as Srdjan.

MUSEUM SUBMISSION 42-2011

The months didn't quite match up. Every sailor, every soldier, and every traveling salesman since the beginning of time knows how to count and at least half of them forget how to on purpose. It's the only way. I was on my second tour. When she wrote me and told me she was pregnant, the first thing I thought was: even my semen doesn't last that long. Damn, I really did love her. For a time anyway. Which is why it was so hard to send that *Dear Jane* letter. She wrote, called, Skyped; swearing it was mine. Then after a few months of silence on my side she confessed it wasn't. Told me who the father really was. Said I was the one she really loved. I'm sending you this letter from her, the one where she asks me to be a father to a child that isn't mine. And to go with it, here's a picture of me with my buddies during my last week in Afghanistan. That's me on the far left.

Does that look like the face of a guy who would take this shit?
I thought about it, though. I'll give her that much.

Bagram Air Force Base, Afghanistan, 2011

Katia

Goran tried both directions, but the clunky metal key wouldn't budge. He leaned closer into the door and tried again. They had just arrived at their hotel in Vienna. It was their last stop after Zagreb and the Croatian coast.

"Why don't you go find her?" Katia asked as he struggled with the lock.

They had gone three days at the coast in Croatia without Katia asking him that question. They had found joy in being together, in walks, in late dinners with a bottle of local wine. Now she asked this to the back of his head.

He turned and stared at her and tried the key again, finally getting it to open.

"Well? I don't understand why. It clearly means something to you. A lot. And you won't talk about it. You still won't. The most obvious thing to do is to reach out to her."

Goran didn't respond as he dropped his bag on the floor. It was the middle of the day, her favorite time to have sex. They both knew this. When they were first going out she would sometimes call or text him between classes and propose that they meet at his place, or hers. She knew he liked this about her. This directness, telling him what she liked and when and how.

"Do you still want to go to the Freud museum?" he asked, looking at the hotel bed and then away from it. "I think we can make it with plenty of time before it closes."

She was silent, hoping for something else. He pulled his phone out of his pocket.

"There's a tram stop at the end of the street that'll take us there," he said.

Katia looked at the books on Freud's shelves, the Greek and Egyptian statuettes, the excerpts from his handwritten manuscripts that went on to become classic works, and the famous divan. She wished she could concentrate on all of it. This was one of the parts of the trip she had most anticipated. This should have been the perfect bookend to their trip, a moment to talk about Freud, and about their families and their pasts. Instead, she was conscious of where Goran was and where he wasn't.

As she walked through the museum Goran was not next to her. In every room of the museum he moved in a different direction than she did. By the fourth room, he had left the room altogether and had not told her where he was going.

Later Katia found him standing outside in the garden. It had turned overcast and slightly chilly; he stood with his hands in his pockets.

"Why have you never gone to Brazil to find out more about your biological mother?"

She didn't answer.

"Are you afraid of what you'll find out?"

"Maybe I am. Is that okay? Can I have my reasons?"

"And those are?"

She looked at him.

"Really, Katia, why don't you go find out about your mother, your real mother and your family? If you want to know so much about someone's past, why not think about your own? You're so brave and yet you haven't even learned Portuguese. You're Brazilian by birth but you don't know anything else about the place, or about your biological family."

She turned her back to him and looked toward the museum.

"We sold our Yugoslavian car here in Vienna. That was the last big thing that was ours. From our life before the war. We stayed a few days in a cheap hotel, just a few blocks from here. Then we got this thick envelope from the US embassy and that fancy visa in our passports. And we left. It was the first time I had ever been on an airplane."

"I'm cold just standing here," she said. "I think I'll go back inside."

"You didn't answer my question."

"We have two days left of our vacation, Goran. I want to try that café we read about downtown and then walk around the museum district before we head out for dinner."

"Yes, we should."

They went back to their hotel room before dinner. Goran stepped into the shower. A few minutes later Katia knocked on the bathroom door and walked in. He had his back to the water with the pressure turned up and the temperature high. He leaned out slightly so he could see her.

Katia removed her clothes, dropped them to the floor and pushed them under the sink with her foot. Without asking him, she stepped into the shower stall. He moved enough for her to fit and they slowly put their arms around each other's waists.

She turned her back to him, and moved closer; she felt him stir. They stayed like this for a moment. Goran kissed the back of her neck and then moved his hands between her legs. Even when she turned to face him, they did not kiss. She began stroking him. He reached out to her.

"No, just let me touch you," she said.

He closed his eyes and let her, his body moving involuntarily, their movements more from need than tenderness.

The next morning was their last full day in Vienna. He awoke to find her with her laptop open. He rubbed his eyes.

"I found tickets online. I got a really good fare."

"What are we talking about?"

"Going to Brazil."

"When are you thinking about it ... I need to check ..."

"I bought them. For me."

"You already bought your ticket?"

"Yes. It's time. Like you said, I need to do this."

"Do you want me to join you?"

She focused on her laptop screen and did not answer.

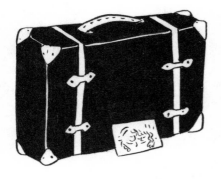

MUSEUM SUBMISSION 2-2010

My mother had always told me she was an orphan, and had no brothers and sisters. She said my father had been a doctor and that he died in a car accident before I was born. It was just the two of us.

One day I came home from school for lunch like I always did and there were two strangers sitting on our couch. My mother said she had something to tell me. She said that these two people were my grandparents. That she and my father had joined the guerrilla movement in the 1970s. And that then she got pregnant with me.

The guerrilla leaders told her she had to get an abortion. How could a revolutionary fighting for the Movement in the Amazon region have a baby? She was supposed to go to the nearby town to a midwife who would perform the abortion, but instead she bought a bus ticket in the direction of São Paulo. Eventually she stopped in the small town I grew up in. She found a priest who helped her out with a place to live and got her a job as a nurse.

While she was telling me all this I kept thinking about the lunch that was waiting for us on the table. I looked at the old people in front of me. I wanted them to leave and take this story with them. And yet I also wanted to know everything about them, and about my father.

My father was a doctor. That part was true. He was a boy from the city and he spent his last days being hunted down by the military in a swamp, probably dehydrated and dysenteric. They never found his body.

For years my mother wondered if the secret police would find us, and take me away and torture her.

I walked over to the couch where my grandparents were sitting and let them hold me. My grandmother cried and said my name over and over like she was trying to memorize it.

My grandparents stayed a few days that first time and from then on we saw them every few months. They became part of our lives.

After they left that first time, my mother looked sad. She said she wanted me to know how much she loved my father, and that she felt guilty every day for leaving him like that.

This is the small suitcase my mother had with her when she got on the bus that day and left my father behind. And this is a picture of the two of them just before they went for guerrilla training in Cuba. They look happy.

I think that he would have been a good father.

São Paulo, Brazil, 2010

Tyler

Tyler had resisted telling his therapist more about Afghanistan and about Cole. He could tell she was desperate when she finally said this: *Tell me about a typical day when you were deployed in Afghanistan.* It sounded like she had pulled it straight out of her textbook.

"I don't know if there was such thing as a typical day over there," he said. "But I do think about this day."

And then he told her.

It was late, a cool fall night in Mazari Sharif, three days closer to the end of his last tour of duty, and just a month after Cole had left. Although Tyler and Cole weren't stationed together, at least he felt like he had someone he knew somewhere close by. Somebody who knew where he came from and somebody he could find again when he went home. Somebody who would understand Afghanistan. They managed to hang out a few times during R&R.

That day, his unit had been on patrol around a clinic the US government was building for one of the small towns where Taliban were present. After the patrol, Tyler worked out in their makeshift gym and was on his way to shower.

The hallway in his barracks was quiet. It smelled of men's sweat mixed with antiseptic cleaning fluid. It was stuffy, as if the windows were kept closed too much. The muffled sound of heavy metal music came from one of the rooms at the other end of hall. There was no one else in the hallway.

On his way to the shower, Tyler opened the door to the supply room to get some soap and saw a stocky soldier, wearing nothing but his briefs, sitting on a stool and holding a gun with the barrel in his mouth. Tyler stopped, his hand still on the doorknob. There was a blurry moment of remembering his suicide prevention training at the police academy. He recognized the soldier: Abrams. Tyler didn't know him well but he knew who he was.

Abrams looked up at him. Tyler stepped quickly into the small room and closed the door behind him.

"Sorry to be coming in right now, I just ..." Tyler said, trying to act as if he had really seen nothing.

"Get the fuck out," Abrams said.

Tyler saw that Abrams' face was red, and his eyes bloodshot; he might have been drinking, or using drugs, or both. Abrams smelled sour, like congealed sweat mixed with stale beer. Tyler stood in front of him, but looked to his side as if focusing on finding the soap he had originally come in for.

"Look, Abrams, I'm not going to try and talk you out of anything, okay? But here's the deal. I was a cop in Austin before I came here. We had to bury one of our patrolmen. Left duty one day, drove his truck way out into the countryside on the way to Fredericksburg. Took out his official issue .38, put it in his mouth, and pulled the trigger. Two little kids, and a wife who adored him."

Tyler paused to look at Abrams.

"He's gone, of course. Whatever you believe about heaven or an afterlife or whatnot, he's not here. But they're still here. His little boy and girl couldn't even see their father's body. They were so little they couldn't understand that inside that big box everyone was crying around was what was left of their father. For them, Daddy had just gone away and they kept asking when he would come back."

He looked at Abrams a moment to see where his hand was. He continued to hold the gun but was pointing it at the ground.

"So, if you can tell me you don't have a mom or a wife or a best friend or a father or somebody back there who is waiting for you to come home in one piece, well then I'll walk out and pretend I never saw you here."

"Fuck you."

"I'll take that as a yes. You do have a mother, and a best friend. A wife maybe. Kids?"

Tyler saw the wedding ring on Abrams' hand.

For an indeterminately long time they just stayed like that, Abrams with the gun in his hand, pointing it to the ground, and Tyler looking at him and then away. Tyler sighed loudly enough to break the silence. Abrams looked up at him, as if he were a child giving in to a patient parent. Abrams shook his head and held out his hand for Tyler to take the gun.

Tyler tried to look into Abrams' eyes again but Abrams avoided him.

He lost track of how much time passed; seconds, a few minutes, maybe longer.

The door opened. It was the platoon sergeant. He stepped inside and looked at the two soldiers.

"Sorry to intrude, fellows. Everything okay?" the sergeant said, looking at Tyler and at the gun in his hand, and at Abrams sitting in his briefs.

"Yessir," Tyler said. "I was just about to clean my gun and then Abrams came in to get something and we started talking. Hard to find quiet around here."

"I know about that," the sergeant said and took a towel and turned to leave.

"As you were," the sergeant said and walked out.

"Yessir," Tyler responded, putting the gun into one of the pockets of his work-out pants.

As soon as the door was closed, Tyler said, "Can I give it back to you? Are we okay?"

Abrams looked up at him and this time Tyler got a good look at him. He had broad shoulders, and a large scar just under the right side of his chin. It was difficult to look at him without staring at the scar chiseled into his rock-like face.

"Look Abrams, if you ever want to talk, come find me, alright? I reckon we've all had these days. We're just not supposed to talk about it."

Abrams did not look back at him.

Tyler hesitated to leave him alone; he remembered his police training regarding suicide attempts. He knew he should stay close. But he could also see how ashamed Abrams was. Tyler thought he might be causing more harm than good by staying.

"Get the fuck out of here," Abrams said.

Tyler thought about asking why. About what was on his mind. But he didn't need to. It was obvious. Because they had to shoot at women and children and men who most of the time were doing nothing more dangerous than herding goats. Because men whose mothers wiped their forehead when they had fevers and made them macaroni and cheese and whose fathers tossed them up in the air and bear-hugged them when they scored the winning run had trouble shooting at grandmothers and children no matter how much the technology of war had changed. Because they had to leave wives and girlfriends and babies behind and wondered if they'd be able to make their mortgage on soldier's pay. Because they knew the names of places that most Americans couldn't find on a map and didn't care to.

Tyler opened the door and walked out, hoping that he was doing the right thing.

Tyler saw Abrams only once more, a few days before he started the journey home, in front of the mess tent. Tyler saw Abrams before he noticed him. He noted again that Abrams was a well-built man with a face that looked like it could turn into rage in an instant. Tyler had seen such men when he was a police officer; it was usually responding to an incident of domestic violence.

"Corporal Nielsen," Abrams said, looking Tyler in the eyes.

"Private Abrams," Tyler said, matching his gaze.

◆ ◆ ◆

"So you saved a soldier who was going to kill himself, but you lost a fellow police officer and you lost Cole. What do you ...?"

"I didn't really know that patrolman. I had just joined the force a few months before it happened and I had seen him at roll call now and then. Met his family at a barbecue. Sweet kids. Both younger than Sammy is now."

"Then your friend Cole did the same thing."

"Yeah."

"What do you think about when you think about Cole killing himself?"

He turned away from her for a moment and then turned back to face her.

"I'm angry at him, and at myself. At him because we're still here. His mother is still here. I'm still here. She'll walk around with that empty space next to her for as long as she lives. And I'm mad that I don't have him to talk to about Afghanistan. Someone who knows what it's like to be there and then to be back here.

"He was going to be my anchor here. Somebody I could call when no one else around me got it, you know. Now it's like fuck you, man. Fuck you, Cole. I could really use you now. The truth? I want to tell him that he was a coward. That we're all suffering here. We're all alone. We're all living with these ghosts and doubts.

"And then I cry a little and I feel so, so sorry for him. And I wonder why I didn't do more. Like why didn't I just go to his place instead of calling. Just show up at his door and drag him out of his house or whatever and get him to talk to me."

He turned away from her and rubbed his eyes.

"You know you couldn't have stopped him, right?"

"Maybe I could have. He might have tried it again, but maybe I could have slowed it down. Shit, I've seen enough on patrol in Afghanistan. And here for that matter. I know that. But maybe he would have lasted a little longer. Maybe that would have been enough. It's not like you save somebody forever. You just save them for another day is how I look at it."

"But he decided to commit suicide. That was *his* decision. It's important for you to remember that."

"You remember I told you he was in his car when he did it, on the highway late at night? He was at I-10 right by the exit for 71. I'm not sure you know where that is. Are you from here?"

"I just moved here a few months ago."

"Well, that 71 is the same Highway 71 as here in town. It becomes Ben White Boulevard. Coming from Houston, you take I-10 and then turn on Highway 71 to come to Austin and Bastrop. He told his mom he was on his way to see me. That was the day he killed himself. He was forty-five minutes away, right there on the side of the road. Halfway to my place. To come and talk to me."

MUSEUM SUBMISSION 30-2013

He's a musician living in Austin. I am too. But I do studio work, so I don't travel like he does.

He had a hit some years back, one you've probably heard, and since then he's been able to make a living at it. Doesn't have to wait tables like I do. But it means he has to travel all the time, Nashville, Houston, Atlanta, Chicago, Baltimore.

We made it a contest to see if we could stay faithful with him away so much. It was our running joke so that it didn't destroy us. We both have enough years on the road behind us. Let's just say we have children old enough to buy their own weed and that we've both been through this story before. I see the women looking at him during the show. And he sees the guys in his band looking at me, so I guess it evens out.

We made it a year together. We were going for our second.

We didn't really say it would mean the end if we couldn't resist. But we both knew from experience that cheating is hard to live through.

It doesn't really matter who gave in first. To that look across the room at the end of the show. You know, when it's closing time and you think about the empty hotel bed waiting for you. And then you walk outside and it's so dark that the streetlights barely make a dint. And suddenly that unfamiliar face and those unfamiliar lips and those unfamiliar hands make their way down your body and instantly become known.

We got along well. Our kids said we belonged together. I think they were relieved with the idea that we might be there to care for each other when we got old so they didn't have to.

If we could just forget it, just leave it to the dark and endless night. There's got to be a way that cheating doesn't have to be cheating and loving can still be true.

That's from a song I wrote. I was probably trying too hard to be poetic about what was nothing more than another shitty break-up.

This is the only shirt he left in my closet. One of his cool singer-songwriter shirts. I couldn't bear his smell on it and then after a time I couldn't detect his smell on it anymore, and I couldn't bear that either. So I wrote a song about him, and I'm sending you the words and the shirt. Maybe I should have called him instead. Maybe I still will. Maybe I'm sending this to test how those words feel written on a page and what they might feel like if I said them out loud.

Austin, Texas, USA, 2013

Katia

It was her third week of Portuguese class in Rio de Janeiro. The teacher played a song on his laptop.

"Escute esta letra," the teacher said. *Listen to the words to this one.*

Cariocas são bonitos
Cariocas são bacanas
Cariocas são sacanas
Cariocas são dourados
Cariocas são modernos
Cariocas são espertos
Cariocas não gostam de dias nublados ...
Cariocas não gostam de sinal fechado ...

The singer reiterated what everyone knows about people from Rio de Janeiro: that they are beautiful, cool, devious, clever, tan, hip. And they don't like cloudy days. Nor stopping for red lights. As she understood this last part, Katia felt a wave of sadness. The teacher noticed her expression.

"Katia, quer dizer alguma coisa sobre a musica?" Felipe, the teacher, said slowly, pronouncing each word clearly. *Do you want to say something about the song?*

"*Nada, não,*" she answered.

The class was four women including Katia, and two men. All were slightly older than Katia. Four worked for multinational corporations, one for the British consulate. Katia guessed they were all charmed by Felipe. He seemed to be the Carioca-prototype the song spoke of: funny and cute, with a little boy's smile even though he was probably about Katia's age, and skin the color of olives.

◆ ◆ ◆

Her father, Kevin, had insisted on taking Katia to the airport for her flight to Rio three weeks earlier. He drove the two-and-a-half hours from Madison to Chicago. Katia insisted he didn't need to, but he said he wanted to, and that he had other people he wanted to see in Chicago. They had a long lunch together after he arrived and then began their drive to Chicago O'Hare for her overnight flight. The lunch conversation had covered Brazilian politics. Kevin was a sociology professor, and had done field work in Brazil. He had stories to tell.

Later, in the car, his tone shifted.

"Katia, every day I worry that we should have taken you on this trip years ago. Gone with you. But we couldn't. We just couldn't. I couldn't anyway."

"I'm not angry, Kevin. I wasn't ready until now either. I may not find anyone who can tell me anything, but I feel I need to try to understand something about where I'm from."

"You asked me a long time ago, about that day, the day Kyle was killed. And I didn't answer. It wasn't because you weren't ready to hear. It's because I couldn't talk about it with you."

Kevin took a long breath. She understood now why he was here and why he had waited to have this conversation in the car. His eyes focused on the highway.

"Kyle was just becoming ... I don't know how to describe it ... aware. He was at that amazing two-year-old stage where they pick up everything. Everyday they master some new concept or new word. And he was doing that in English *and* Portuguese. Small stuff, but amazing to parents. Some days, after I picked him up from day care, we'd go to a park close to our apartment. I would remind myself not to squeeze his hand so tightly. I lived in panic. You'll see how the traffic is in Rio, how the drivers keep going through the intersection even after a signal turns red. He loved to take off running. So I worried.

"That day after I picked him up from his day care, he kept saying '*Parque*, Daddy. Parque, parque now.' I was hoping to convince him to go back to our apartment and have his afternoon nap so I could work. But he kept saying it. 'Parque, now.'

"That was something new for him—the meaning of now and later. It was like Kyle understood for the first time when he was being put off, you know. He kept saying 'now.' And it seemed ridiculous, on such a sunny day, not to go to the park.

"So I said okay and Kyle said 'Parque, now!' with his happy voice. Then we walked to the place where we had to cross the main road to get to Lagoa. I mean, we crossed there nearly every day.

"Kyle was carrying a wooden figure made out of Popsicle sticks that he made at his daycare in one hand and holding my hand with the other. While we waited for the signal to change, I asked him to show me what he had made and he held it up for me to see. I asked him what color at it was and he said, 'wed.' And I said, 'yeah, it's red.' And then he said it in Portuguese too: '*Vermelho*.'"

Kevin paused as if to take another slow breath. Katia looked at him but he did not turn to meet her eyes.

"The light turned red for pedestrians to cross. A few drivers accelerated through the signal like they do all the time in Rio, until finally the traffic stopped. When we stepped into the intersection, Kyle dropped the Popsicle stick man. I took a step backwards to pick it up. Then I let go of his hand for just that second, it was just that quick ... and that's when the motorcycle ..."

Kevin stopped for a moment. She turned to face him again, and again he did not meet her eyes.

"I'm so sorry, Kevin, I can't even imagine."

"No, Katia, I'm the one who's sorry. That's a long time ago and the hurt will always be there, I think. But the other part of it all is that I wasn't ready when your mother came home saying there was a baby who needed a family. I just wasn't ready for you to be this lovely baby girl and to be ours. Some days I feel like I missed all those moments when you were changing right before our eyes because I was so stuck in my own pain."

Katia knew the effort he had put into saying all this. She had lived through the years of silence and the diversionary conversations.

"Thank you for telling me this. I mean it." A part of her thought: *You're a few years late.*

They passed a few minutes of silence before they arrived at O'Hare. When they pulled up in the passenger drop-off area, Kevin got out of the car and hugged Katia for longer than he usually did.

"Write us, okay? An email, text message. Call now and then. You know we love you."

"Of course."

◆ ◆ ◆

Those first weeks in Rio de Janeiro, Katia had a half day of language classes every day. She ran or went for long walks on the oceanfront in Ipanema. She read. She kept up with emails. At night she ate in restaurants she found online. She usually brought a book with her to fill the empty space.

Katia knew almost no one in the city; she had contacted two people whose names her mother had given her, people who might be able to tell her how to find her birth family. They had given her addresses and phone numbers. She kept the information in a small notebook, waiting for when she was ready. In her head she practiced phrases in Portuguese of how she would introduce herself and what she would ask them.

Through one of her professors back in Chicago, Katia had gotten in touch with an NGO that worked with survivors of torture, mostly from the military dictatorship, but also victims of police torture. They sent her dates of upcoming seminars they were organizing and they asked about Katia's own past and what she knew about her mother.

One afternoon, after a run on the beach in Ipanema, she stopped at the oceanside kiosk where she often had a coconut water before walking back to her rented apartment. She sat down at a table and looked at the ocean. A man came up to her. She guessed by his tucked in polo shirt that he was American.

"*Oi, tudo bem?*" he asked, using what Katia guessed was his only phrase of Portuguese.

"*Tudo. E voce?*" she said. With this much Portuguese, she could pass as fluent.

"Do you speak English?" the man said slowly, his accent confirming that he was American.

"Yes, I do."

"Listen, me and my buddies are going to a party later. Are you, uh, working? I mean, you up for some partying with me?"

"No, no thanks."

"Is there someplace you normally work? A club around here where I could find you and, you know, hook up?"

"No. I'm not a prostitute. Maybe you and your buddies could work on your dating skills so you wouldn't have to pay."

"Sorry, my bad," the man said and walked away before Katia could say anything else.

The woman who ran the kiosk heard part of the conversation and came over to Katia after the man had walked away. Like Katia, the woman was black and had a long afro; she was probably ten years older than Katia.

"*Esta tudo bem, querida?*"

"This asshole thought I was a prostitute," Katia answered in Portuguese.

"It happens to me sometimes, too."

"A guy would never do that in the US, or at least, if he did, he would worry about getting arrested."

"We're *mulatas, querida*, in a country where sex work is legal. Some guys, if we don't look like a maid or a nanny, think we're prostitutes."

Katia looked at the woman.

"I'm not going to judge, *amiga*. If a woman from a favela wants to have sex for money with gringos instead of being a maid in some rich people's apartment in Ipanema, who am I to judge?"

One afternoon after Portuguese class, Katia saw that Felipe was carrying a yoga mat rolled up under his arm. He strapped it on the back of his motorcycle.

"Where do you do yoga?" she asked him in English.

"At a place just across the street from the botanical gardens, the Jockey Club."

"Do you think they have any openings?"

"I'm sure they do. I can take you now if you want to see the place and ask."

Katia climbed on the back of his motorcycle for the short ride. She signed up for a class, thanked Felipe for the introduction, and made her way back to her apartment by taxi while he went to his class.

A few days later, one of Felipe's regular yoga sessions was cancelled and he ended up in the same class as Katia. They chatted a little before the class, and then set up their mats.

She was distracted afterwards. Yoga always gave her the sensation of having just woken up from a fabulous nap. Felipe's voice felt intrusive.

"You want a ride? I'm heading in the direction of Copacabana," Felipe said in Portuguese, as they left the yoga studio.

"Sure, I'm staying in Ipanema, if it's not out of your way."

"It's right on the way. If you want, we can get a juice or something to eat. Do you know Bibi's?"

She accepted.

"Do you want to speak in Portuguese now? Or English?" he asked her in English as they sat down in the small juice bar.

"We could, but my brain is a bit weary from speaking Portuguese all day. Is English okay?"

"Of course."

Although he was fluent in English, his accent came out strongly in a few words.

"How long have you taught Portuguese?"

"This is my second year with the school. Part of the time I teach Portuguese to foreigners and part of the time I teach English to Brazilians. I'm working on a master's in cultural production—theater, events, museums, and things like that. Teaching pays the bills until I finish and find a job doing what I really want to do.

"What brings you to Brazil? You're in graduate school too, you said."

"I'm doing a master's in psychology, trauma counseling. I have one more year until I finish. And I'm here because technically I'm from here. I was born in Rio to a Brazilian family. My biological mother was killed right after I was born and I was adopted by an American family when I was a week old. So, I had never been here before and it was time. I've never met anyone from my biological family. My parents, I mean my adoptive parents, never knew them. I hope I'll be able to find them. But I'd like to be able to talk to them in Portuguese."

"So you're a Carioca."

"I suppose."

"Wow, that must be strange to be here for the first time since you were a baby."

He took a sip from his juice.

"You're doing this alone?"

"Yeah, why not?"

"I don't know, it seems like something to share with your parents, the ones who adopted you, or your boyfriend, or a good friend."

"Maybe it's an American thing. We like to do everything on our own."

"Do you have a boyfriend? If that's okay to ask."

"Or girlfriend," she said.

"I think you like guys."

"Maybe both," she said.

She looked away from him, and dangled her straw and was aware of his eyes on her in a way that she liked.

"Yeah, I have a boyfriend, in Chicago, where I live.

Goran just finished his PhD and has a teaching position at DePaul, one of the universities in Chicago. He's supposed to be coming for a week to be here for part of this with me. He said he would, anyway. We'll see. It's a long story."

"Tell me. I mean if you want."

She told Felipe about the museum and about Goran's past.

"Wow, I want to see this museum," Felipe said. "It's a great idea really, a museum to talk about, in Portuguese we'd call it *desamor*. I don't know how to say that in English. Being out of love, I guess. So, will he go find the woman from back in the war?"

"I don't know. He says there's no reason to, that she's just a girl he barely knew from nearly twenty years ago."

"That's a pretty amazing coincidence."

"Yeah, but then it led to this stupid fight between us. We both ended up more or less calling the other a coward for not being brave enough to connect to our past."

"So you mean he hasn't gone to find the woman?"

"Not that I know of."

"But you're here looking for your past. So who's the coward?"

"I still haven't had the courage to contact my family yet."

"You've only been here a few weeks, right? You have a little way to go on your Portuguese. Although it's getting better fast."

"You're just saying that to be on my side."

"Absolutely," he said, and smiled.

She took a sip from her juice and glanced at him again. The energy from yoga was still in her head and she felt like she could say these things, like she needed to.

"This all happened right when it started to feel like it

was the real thing with Goran, you know, like he's *it*. Like we wanted to be together. That's when he saw that letter in the museum and he got all defensive about it and he wouldn't talk to me and pulled away. What's the word for that in Portuguese? You taught it to us. *Azar?*"

"Yeah, that's it," he said. "Destiny. Bad luck. Bummer."

She looked away from Felipe, toward the street.

"What do you know about your Brazilian family?"

"That my mother was from a favela, Santa Marta, and that she was killed in gang violence."

"That's not an easy story for parents to tell their adopted daughter."

"No. Not without years of therapy."

"You mean for them, or you?"

"Me for sure. I don't know if they ever went. If they did they never told me."

For a brief moment Felipe dropped his perpetual smile.

"Have you been to a favela?" he said.

"I'm still trying to get my courage up."

He nodded; a semblance of his smile returned.

"I'll take you if you want. I'm working on this project in a favela called Nova Holanda with some students from there. They'd be super-curious about you."

She nodded.

"What about Santa Marta?" she asked. "Would you go there with me?"

"Yeah, sure."

"Thank you. Hey, do you mind if we get the check?"

Felipe nodded, and he looked at her in a way that made Katia think he liked her and wanted her to know it, and she gave him a look that she hoped said the same.

They paid their bill and he dropped her off at her apartment.

Later that night she received a text message from Goran. He would come. Katia hadn't asked him to but he insisted. She texted him back a few minutes later: *I'm glad you're coming. I miss you. I'll meet you at the airport.*

She was only sure about the last part.

MUSEUM SUBMISSION 97-2010

He was everything to me. He cared for me, cooked for me, took me to the park, picked me up at ballet class, let me play *Pretty, Pretty Princess* with him. You spin the pointer to win jewelry and the one who gets all the pieces, including the tiara, wins. My friends loved that, especially when he won and he had all the princess jewelry on. We laughed so hard. I can still remember we all threw ourselves on my bed in laughter when my father wore the tiara.

It was just the two of us all those years after my mother left and moved to Australia. Then he met my stepmother. It's such a horrible word.

I was twelve when it happened. I was smart enough to be critical of those Grimm brothers' ideas of what a stepmother was. But things started to happen. He was not there for me. She wanted him all for herself and he wanted to be everything to her.

I swear I tried. It felt so cliché to hate my stepmother and yet there it is. All that was missing was for her to lure me into the woods and put me into a deep sleep.

But she was more subtle than that. I'm not sure she even knew she was doing it. She pushed his friends away and then me. I became the outsider in my childhood home.

I grew up and left. The twosome that my father and I had been all that time was gone.

I still see my father and stepmother, and it doesn't hurt as much as it used to. They more or less accept me as I am. Or maybe it's just that they ignore me as I am.

Still, something was lost along the way and I can't help but think that it was taken from me without so much as an acknowledgment. I think there must be a tribe somewhere, maybe the one in the highlands in Central Africa where babies suck on their father's nipples and are as likely to call out for their fathers as for their mothers. I bet they have a ritual for cases like mine. Where daughters of single fathers walk their fathers down the aisle and give them away or something like that.

In that tribe, I imagine that the daughters get to make their fathers wear a princess gown and a tiara. In case anyone wants to invent that ritual, I'm sending you the game, the old *Pretty, Pretty Princess* game that my father used to play with me. Back when he was mine.

Vancouver, Canada, 2010

Tyler

"I sometimes forget that you're a police officer until I see you in uniform," Carla said, as he was walking out of his apartment and she was arriving at hers.

"Hey. I had to make a quick stop before heading back to the station."

"It suits you. The uniform."

She smiled in a way that both made him embarrassed and at the same time made him want to stay right there, feeling her look at him.

"I'm kind of running late. I have to drop something off back at the station, and then get Sammy," he said.

"Sure. It was good ...," she started.

"Yeah," he said, interrupting her. "Hey, do you wanna ... You know it's gotten warmer and I've been thinking of taking Sammy to Barton Springs. You guys want to come along?"

◆ ◆ ◆

The day at Barton Springs followed the rhythm of the boys: swimming, playing around the natural pool, swimming again, eating, swimming some more, then dropping from exhaustion. Every time Carla and Tyler started a conversation, one of the boys needed something. They wanted to be tossed up in the air or into the water, they wanted an ice-cream cone or a drink, or they needed to go to the restroom.

After an early dinner in Austin, both boys fell asleep in the car during the drive back to Bastrop.

"Why don't you come up for a few minutes," she said.

"Yeah, sure, for a few minutes. I'll get Sammy," he said.

"Want to put him in on the couch in Joaquin's room?"

These were innocuous enough questions from her. But Tyler thought he caught in her eyes a slight squint, and thought he heard a hushed tone in her voice, both of which hinted that she was leading them somewhere he wanted to follow. At the very least he was curious of where it might go.

He put Sammy gently down on the small couch in Joaquin's room, looking at him for a moment to check if he was still sound asleep.

Tyler walked from Joaquin's bedroom to the living room. He stood at the edge of the living room, as if trying to figure out where to rest his eyes, and to make it clear with his body that he was not really staying, not for long anyway. Carla had put a bottle of wine out and begun pouring for them both. He continued to stand in the same place.

"You want to sit down or ...?" she asked.

"Yeah," he said, his voice distracted.

"Am I getting you in trouble?" she said.

"Probably."

His voice was serious. He looked toward the door and then toward the front window.

"Yes," he said, firmly now, walking to the front of the couch and sitting down just at the edge of it.

"Should you leave?" she asked.

"Do you want me to?" he asked, still not looking at her, still serious.

She waited until he turned toward her. Then she shook her head and gave away the beginning of a smile.

He sat back on the couch and reached for the glass of wine she was now holding out for him.

"Thanks," he said. "It's just that the instructions were clear between the shelter and the sheriff's department. I'm not supposed to hang out with you."

He continued to look straight ahead; he could feel her gaze on him.

"Cheers," she said, and clinked her glass to his. "To breaking rules that are okay to break sometimes."

"Okay, cheers to that."

Carla was close enough that Tyler could smell the fresh scent of river water on her. He knew he needed to keep his job even more now that he had Sammy to look out for. As he was thinking this, Carla kissed him, gently at first, then more forcefully. He put his glass down on the coffee table and reached for her.

"Hey," she said, "let's make sure they're asleep."

Holding his hand, she led him down the short hallway. They stuck their heads into Joaquin's room and saw the boys sleeping soundly. Carla closed the door gently, and turned back to him.

Tyler followed her to her bedroom and she turned on a lamp on her nightstand. Carla pulled off her dress, leaving only her bikini bottoms on. He took off his shirt and stood before her. He reached his hand down her back just inside her pants.

"Take them off," she ordered.

His head rushed with what would happen next; where lips and tongues and hands would go. Where the two of them might go. He was new at this—what it took to have even the briefest moments of calm or lust with two four-year-old boys in stand-by mode just down the hall. He thought for a moment of phrases he wanted to whisper to her as she reached for him and he reached for her. Of sounds he wanted to make and wanted her to know he was making because of her.

As he was lost in that thought, he heard a noise. At first it seemed like a television in a neighboring apartment. Then it became louder.

"Mommy. Mommy."

There was silence and then it started again.

"Mommy. Mommy."

It was not a scream; it was plaintive.

Tyler and Carla listened, hoping and wishing that it would go away.

"Mommy. I feel sick."

Carla grabbed a batik-print robe from the back of her door and put it on.

"I'll go see what it is," she said.

She left, and a moment later he heard her open the door to Joaquin's room.

"Hey, honey, what's the matter?"

It was then that Tyler took in Carla's room. It had a futon on a low wooden frame, and a simple nightstand in similar dark wood on one side. She'd hung an Asian-print cloth over the side of the non-descript chair in the corner. On the dresser he saw her nametag from Breckenridge Hospital and the colored bead necklaces she often wore. Seeing it all, he pushed against the thought that he shouldn't be here.

When she didn't come back immediately, Tyler put on his shirt and went to the door of Joaquin's room. He saw Carla's hand on Joaquin's head and could tell by the smell that Joaquin had vomited. Sammy was still sleeping soundly.

"I'll get a towel," Tyler said.

Carla looked back at him.

"Grab the hand towel in the bathroom."

Tyler found it, wet it slightly, and brought it to her.

"Thanks," she said.

"Want me to bring a bucket and some water?"

"Yes, please. There are more towels under his sink. Can you bring a couple more? And wet one more of them like you did this one. The bucket is under the kitchen sink."

"Ok."

Tyler came back with the towels and the bucket.

"Too much Mexican food, I guess, plus he probably swallowed half of Barton Springs," Carla said, trying to wrap the towels together and cleaning up as much as she could. "Nothing serious. Could you stay here while I get some clean sheets and a glass of water for Joaquin?"

"Sure."

Tyler sat on the edge of Joaquin's bed. Joaquin seemed to have already fallen asleep again. The smell started to dissipate. Tyler wondered if Sammy would find this situation strange. Carla came back a moment later with some cleaning towels, Lysol, and a sheet.

"I'll clean the rest of the carpet and you can change the sheets," he said.

"Thanks."

She helped Joaquin to the floor and gave him some water while she changed the sheet and Tyler cleaned the floor. Sammy began to stir.

"What happened?" Sammy said in a sleepy voice.

"Hey, kiddo," Tyler said, moving over to him. "You and Joaquin fell asleep in the car so we brought you both in here. Then Joaquin started feeling sick. He threw up so we had to clean up. We'll go home in a little while. I'm just helping Joaquin's mom for a few minutes."

Carla rolled up the soiled sheet, putting the towels inside of it.

"Here, I can take it," Tyler said.

"Just toss it in the washing machine."

He walked to the laundry area next to her kitchen and put the bundle in the machine, when she walked up behind him and held him.

"I hadn't planned on the evening ending this way," Carla said.

Tyler smiled.

"It's okay," he said. "Life with four-year-olds. You know more about it than I do. I should get Sammy in his bed."

"Tell me that we'll resume this," she said.

"I ...," he started. "Of course."

Wednesday morning, Tyler dropped Sammy off at daycare and came back to the apartment to change into his work-out clothes. As he was opening his door, he saw Carla pulling up in her car and watched her step out in green surgical scrubs. She smiled and walked up the stairs to his apartment.

"Hey," she said, moving toward him and almost kissing him, but then stopping.

"Hey," he said.

"You have the morning off?" she asked.

"Yeah, I do. I guess you must be exhausted after the night shift."

"Suddenly full of energy," she said with a powerful stare. "Come over in fifteen minutes."

It was a command, not a question, and he nodded, as if it were out of his control. He showered quickly, put on jeans, a black T-shirt, and flip-flops, and went to her apartment.

She was wearing the same batik-print robe. As he stepped into the apartment, he reached his hands around to grab her ass. He could tell she had nothing on underneath. She pulled his T-shirt off and began kissing his chest. He moved his hands from around her and found the sash to her robe and undid it, sliding his hands underneath.

She moved away slightly as she opened his jeans.

"You always go without underwear when you're on duty?" she said.

"I was in a hurry," he said.

"I hope you're not now."

"Nope."

For some amount of time he could not precisely gauge, Tyler didn't notice where their bodies intersected. Afterwards he couldn't remember who set the pace. Or who decided exactly who did what to whom.

◆ ◆ ◆

This became their routine: texting each other in search of moments when the boys were at preschool and when they were both off work.

Saturdays, it was the four of them, and Sundays they were nearly always with their respective families. Some weeknights, they would share a pizza and watch a movie together, or the boys played in Joaquin's room while Tyler and Carla sat on the couch in the living room acting like teenagers: whispering, kissing, and letting their hands slip beneath layers of clothing, ready to withdraw at a moment's notice if they heard one of the boys coming.

Tyler and Carla avoided discussing the difficult things. They didn't talk about her ex, the court case, or when she would move out of the apartment that the women's shelter provided. Or about what would happen if the women's shelter found out about the two of them.

"We deserve this, Tyler," Carla said one night before they fell asleep in her bed, Sammy sleeping in Joaquin's room.

"I'm never sure what I deserve," he said. "But I know I want this."

MUSEUM SUBMISSION 71-2010

He left just like that, said he was going for cigarettes and a newspaper one hot Saturday afternoon and never came back. I tried reaching his folks, other people who knew him. Folks who would know where he was. Not a word. Except a cousin who told me he had done this before.

Nobody knows what he's running to or from. Some's just runners, that's what I figure. One of my daughters, she's at university, told me about your museum. Seemed as good a place as any to send this. Made me wonder if maybe there's a place where some of them meet up. Like, a runners club. Made me wonder if they know about this museum and some of them come to find things, things their ex-lovers and ex-wives send to them. Didn't seem like I should keep this with me, like he's going to come back to me or something. It's a picture of his Daddy and him. His Daddy was a runner too. This is all he has to remember his Daddy by. If runners like him come here and he comes by, and he wants this, you can give it him.

Mobile, Alabama, USA, 2010

Katia

The following Saturday morning Felipe picked her up on his motorcycle and drove to the base of Santa Marta, the favela where her mother was from. Katia had passed by it several times, always looking at it through the tinted window of an air-conditioned taxi. Now, at the bottom, staring up, Katia realized that she was from here.

The houses, improbably stacked on top of one another in what seemed like one huge, interconnected mass of human dwelling, were mostly made of unpainted cement and red cinder blocks. Some were painted white, grey, yellow, or light blue. There was no passage for cars beyond the central plaza. The walkways that went up into Santa Marta were a mixture of dirt trails and cement steps, with wet stains of sewage in some areas. There was laundry hanging from windows and in small patios, and electric wiring that seemed to have reproduced out of control. Satellite dishes atop rooftops were packed closely together.

The residents didn't give Katia and Felipe any special attention. There were boys, some shirtless and in shorts and sandals, and little girls in simple dresses or shorts and tank tops. Some of the men and women had on the worn clothes of deliverymen or maids, others were in shorts and T-shirts. Some wore immaculately pressed shirts and blouses, neatly tucked in, as if they were going to one of the high-rise offices in downtown Rio. All were various shades of black.

As Katia and Felipe climbed, they saw the modern apartment buildings of the middle class below them, and beyond those the brilliant blue of the Atlantic Ocean. It was a cloudless day and the temperature was spring-like. She thought that Felipe was the right guide for this; he seemed to know when to offer information and when to stay quiet.

They found the Baptist church that her mother's friend had given as a reference for finding her biological family. They climbed the flight of stairs to the second floor of the church where a man she took to be the pastor was standing and talking. Felipe spoke to the pastor, who offered a large smile and shook his hand.

"*Tudo bem?*" the pastor said.

The pastor looked to be in his late thirties or early forties. He was clean-shaven, with an extremely short afro. He rubbed his chin and smiled while a girl, who looked about four, pulled on his arm. Katia could see the pastor nodding.

"I know the family," the pastor said in Portuguese. "I remember Fatima."

Katia stepped toward them, as she heard her biological mother's name.

"What's he saying?" she asked Felipe. "I lost the last part."

"He said he knew your grandmother and aunt. He was about twelve when it happened. Your grandmother moved away. She moved back to Bahia, where your family is originally from."

The pastor started talking again, tapping his finger on his lips.

"One of Dona Lidia's sisters lives here," the pastor said in Portuguese. "She would be your great aunt. Her name is Dona Ana. I bet she knows where to find your grandmother. I'll take you to her."

"*Você parece com ela*," the pastor said to Katia slowly, smiling. *You look like her.*

Katia smiled.

"*Você entende português?*" he asked.

"I'm learning. If you speak slowly, I can understand," she replied in her accented Portuguese.

"You have the same hair she did. She hated it. Always straightened it. Same smile too."

Katia and Felipe followed the pastor further up into the favela, making turns that would be difficult to remember on the way back down. The pastor stopped to greet an older woman standing in a doorway and introduced Katia. Katia understood that he mentioned her biological mother's name and she understood something about *os homens*. *Those men.* The woman looked at Katia first with a sad expression and then smiled.

"*Meu Deus. Meu Deus. A filha da Fatima. Pelo amor de Deus*," the woman said and touched Katia's arm.

"You're as beautiful as she was," the woman continued. "Your cousins will be so happy to see you. I can't believe it. *Meu Deus*, I can't believe it."

Katia hugged her.

They continued walking, passing a young couple with a son who looked about two years old squirming in his father's arms.

"Are you surviving the climb?" the pastor asked Katia and Felipe.

"Yes, but I can't imagine doing it every day," Katia managed to say in Portuguese.

"Several times a day," he responded, smiling.

After another five minutes of climbing, they reached a house, virtually the same as all the rest, with a metal door, aluminum frame windows, cinder-block walls and flower-print curtains visible just inside the windows.

The pastor leaned his head around toward the window. "Dona Ana," he called out. "*Está em casa?*"

"I'm coming," the voice said.

A woman opened the door. She was shorter than Katia, but still taller than many of the women they had passed. She seemed to be in her early fifties and wore a simple white skirt and a flowery printed top. Her afro was pulled back with a bright red headwrap.

The pastor pointed to Katia and explained who she was. The woman took a deep breath, and then shook her head and was silent for a long time. She put her hand up to her mouth. Katia wondered for a moment if she might faint or walk away in shock.

"*Meu Deus.* Thanks be to God. It really is you," Dona Ana said, and gave Katia a big hug.

"Let me look at you," she continued, holding Katia's face. "*Diretamente dos States.* I can't believe it. I just can't believe it."

Dona Ana called for her grandchildren to come meet Katia, and invited Felipe, Katia and the pastor inside.

The house was neat, with a striped couch against one wall, a TV and stereo console on another, the TV turned on to a *telenovela*. The grandchildren were outside on the small patio. There was a girl of about twelve, another girl of about fourteen, and a boy of seven or eight. All were thin, neatly dressed, and stood up straight when their grandmother spoke to them. They looked on as Ana explained who Katia was. The house smelled of rice and garlic.

"*Americana?*" the younger of the two girls asked with an incredulous smile. "We have an American cousin?"

The girl stood up and shook Katia's hand. Katia smiled at her and the girl hung at her side for a moment with a large smile on her face.

"I'll leave you here," the pastor said. "You're with family. Welcome home. Stop by on your way down if you want."

Katia looked at them with a smile frozen on her face. Suddenly all the Portuguese she had practiced and learned these past weeks seemed to have escaped her. Felipe shook hands with all of them and gave kisses on the cheek to the women and girls.

Dona Ana invited the two of them to sit down on the couch in the living room and brought them water and then overly sweetened, strong coffee.

Ana reached out for Katia's hand and gazed into her face.

"She loved you so much," Ana said. "*Meu Deus*, it's a miracle to see you here. I don't know what to say ... With all that happened, I never imagined we'd see you again. Do you understand? Does she understand?"

Ana looked toward Felipe as she said this last part.

Katia struggled to block out the sound of the TV and to follow Ana's Portuguese. She leaned forward, as if staring at Ana's mouth would help.

"I don't know where to start ... my sister, that's your grandmother, Lidia, moved away afterwards. After all that, she wanted to leave Rio. Back then the gangs made it hell to live here. It's better now. We still have violence but not like back then. And then after your mother was killed, Lidia needed to leave here. She went back to Bahia. Retirolandia, near Salvador, where some of our family are from. That's where she lives now. It was so hard for her."

Felipe translated to make sure she understood it all; Katia nodded.

"Tell me about my mother," Katia said in English, still nodding, her eyes alight, looking to Felipe to translate. "What was she like?"

"She was so full of life. Beautiful. Just like you. She had

a hard life. Her father, your grandfather, used to beat her, trying to make her stay at home and stay out of trouble. Fatima would come running to me and stay at our house for a few days. Then when it quieted down, she'd go back home."

Ana turned to the oldest granddaughter, the girl of about fourteen, and asked her to check on the rice.

"You will stay for lunch," Ana said.

Katia and Felipe looked at each other and nodded.

"You know," Ana continued. "I think it was all that was happening in your house that was part of why your uncle Julio, that's Fatima's brother, joined the gang. And Fatima just tried to pretend it wasn't happening. We all did. But pretty soon Julio was one of them, guns and all. *Teleguiado.* That's what we call them. Remote-controlled by the gang."

Ana stopped for a moment to call out instructions to her grandchildren to bring the food to the table. Then she excused herself to finish the preparation. Katia and Felipe sat on the couch with the grandson while Ana and the girls finished making lunch.

After an awkward silence, the youngest boy asked Katia if she liked living in the US. She asked Felipe to tell the boy that she didn't have anywhere to compare it to since it's the only place she has lived her life up until now. The boy was distracted for a moment, looking outside, as Felipe translated.

"You ever meet Michael Jackson?" the boy asked her.

"No. Did you?" Katia said, in Portuguese.

The boy laughed.

"He came here to make that video. But I was real little then."

A few minutes later lunch was served. It was the Brazilian staple meal that Katia had had in less sophisticated restaurants: rice, beans, cassava flour, roasted chicken, French fries, and a salad of lettuce, onions, and tomato. Ana made the children wait while Katia and Felipe served themselves.

Felipe continued translating during lunch, holding his fork in midair occasionally as he tried to keep up with Ana and Katia.

"Do you know what happened to your mother?" Ana asked as they sat on the couch after lunch.

"Just that she was killed in the middle of the gang wars," Katia tried to reply.

"She fell in love with a boy from the rival gang. Her brother was so angry at her for that. And her boyfriend was mad at her because she wouldn't renounce her brother. They both wanted her to promise she would never see the other one again. Would have been just like Romeo and Juliet if it wasn't real."

Katia stood up and walked over to the window, still looking toward Ana and waiting for Felipe to help explain.

"You'd wake up in the morning and there would be a body on the ground, a young man killed the night before. Police wouldn't come up into the favela so somebody in the community would take the body down to the morgue in a wheelbarrow."

Ana paused and looked at Katia.

"Your mother loved him so much. Your father, Beto. Everyone called him Blondie after he bleached his hair. As handsome and smooth-talking as they come. All the girls around here wanted to be with him. He had money, and a motorcycle. The police were after him so he couldn't really go anywhere to show it off, but he was rich compared to everyone else around here."

Katia nodded as Felipe translated.

"We all knew something bad was going to happen. Fatima couldn't stay in the middle of that forever."

Katia nodded again. Ana reached over to her and held her hand.

"And now you're back here."

Katia was silent for a moment, feeling the warmth of Dona Ana's hand, trying to make sense of it all, half-listening in Portuguese, seeking to fully understand in English.

"We should go," Katia eventually said, making an excuse. "I'm meeting with some friends of my adoptive parents. But I want to come back. If that's okay. Can I come back another day so we can talk some more? Before I go to Bahia?"

"This is your home, *minha filha*. You can come back anytime you want. Maybe I'll come visit you in the States," Ana said, laughing.

Ana stood up, picked up her mobile phone, and wrote down a number on a piece of paper.

"This is your grandmother Lidia's telephone number in Bahia. She doesn't always pay the bill so sometimes it may be off."

"Thank you for lunch," Katia said, hugging Ana.

Felipe stood up and gave Ana two kisses.

"You really are Brazilian," Felipe said in English, as they walked down the steps they had come up. "Carioca at that. The girl from Santa Marta."

Here was another reason Felipe was a great guide: he didn't ask her about why she felt the need to leave all of the sudden.

"I don't think I ever really believed it. I did, but at the same time it sometimes felt like a fairytale my parents told me."

She looked at Felipe.

"Thank you for coming with me."

"No problem."

When they reached the bottom, they climbed on his motorcycle and he looked back at her.

"You feel like doing something? Or do you want to be on your own for a while?" Felipe said.

"I think I need to be alone."

He nodded.

"Goran arrives Monday," she said.

She thought she saw a look of disappointment on Felipe's face.

"Great. I look forward to meeting him. I mean, if you're going to be social while he's here. I understand if you don't want to be."

"Of course," Katia said.

Felipe started the motorcycle and drove Katia back to her apartment.

◆ ◆ ◆

At the arrivals gate at the Rio airport that Monday morning Katia and Goran embraced like they meant it. They were glad to see each other. No matter the tension these past weeks, Goran's smell and his mouth on hers made it all fall away.

They took a taxi back to her apartment, stuck in the morning traffic much of the way, holding hands in the back seat. She told him about the visit to the favela, about her Portuguese classes, about her impressions of Rio.

When they arrived at her apartment, he dropped his bag on the floor and they reached for the other's clothes like they used to whenever they arrived in a hotel, or after they'd been away from each other for a few days. This temporary apartment with the faintest smell of ocean air and the Rio morning light coming through the slightly opened shutters made her feel like they were different versions of themselves. Happier, more forgiving versions.

They slept afterwards. She awoke when the alarm on her phone went off and she got up to shower and dress, leaving him sleeping. She returned to the bed and kissed him gently. He slowly opened his eyes.

"Hey. I have my Portuguese class. I have to get going."

"Can't you miss it today?" he said, his voice sleepy.

"I paid a lot for it and I really need to practice as much as I can. I'll be back in a few hours. Get some rest and we'll go out later. Text me if you need anything. There's food in refrigerator or you can go to the main street and grab something. I left the extra key by the phone if you want to go out."

She ran her hand through his hair.

"I'm glad you're here."

"Are you?" he said.

"Yes, Goran. Of course I am."

"We've hardly spoken these last days and I just arrived and now you're going to class."

"I didn't call because I knew you were coming. Besides, I didn't see you trying to call me these last few weeks."

"Katia ..."

"Goran. I'm glad you're here. Really I am. I'll see you in a few hours. Get some rest."

"You paid for your class. And I paid for the airfare."

She wanted to call him a dick. She wanted to ask him why he had come all this way just to treat her like this. But she wanted it to work. She wanted to avoid another argument if at all possible.

"I'll be back around four and we'll go out. Thank you for being here. Really."

❖ ❖ ❖

Between her classes they went to the beach, the botanical gardens, the museums. They made love mostly late at night, after the *caipirinhas* had taken effect and without much talking. One morning, she woke him up with the tenderness they used to have, with that feeling that all they needed was in this small apartment and in their bed and at the point where their bodies intersected. She thought he felt this too, at least for those few minutes.

A few nights after he arrived, she'd arranged to go out with Felipe and two of the women in her Portuguese class. Felipe called her to the dance floor. As she moved next to him, feeling his hands briefly hold her hips, she felt Goran watching. His stare felt cold. She remembered when they first started going out. If they went out dancing and she danced with other men, he would watch her, but with a different look. He told her then that he found it intriguing. Back then she would tell him to stop watching and get his ass up and on the dance floor with her.

She thought about Goran even as she danced with Felipe. There was so much she wanted to tell him. But feeling his look on her, this angry look, this possessive look, Katia wasn't sure she wanted to tell him anything. She pulled herself out of her thoughts and smiled at Felipe as she spun and moved her hips in a way she thought the Brazilian version of herself should.

On the taxi on the way back from dancing, Katia told Goran about her plans to go see her Brazilian family in Bahia.

"I thought we were going to your grandmother's together. Wasn't that part of me coming?"

"I just got the information from a relative here about where my grandmother lives. It takes a whole day to get there between flying and driving and then a whole day to get back. I have a week off from my Portuguese class coming up so I decided to go then. I knew you only had a short time here. We'll go see my mother's aunt in the favela where I was born instead. She's looking forward to meeting you."

"So you've already met the family here in Rio and you'll go to the family in Bahia by yourself. Why did I come, Katia? I mean ..."

"Wasn't being with me the reason?"

"You said you wanted me to be here for this."

"It's my past and my family, Goran. It's something I needed to do and something I wanted your support for. I don't have a script of how it's going to happen. I'm not waiting for you to give me permission for each ... it's not ..."

"It feels like I don't need to be here."

"Goran, please, it's not like I had surgery or something and needed you at the hospital to take me home. I needed your support. That's why you're here. Just talking with me about it and being here. That's what I need."

She leaned her head on his shoulder in the back seat of the taxi that took them back to her apartment. He did not lean his head toward her.

As the *caipirinhas* buzzed in her head she couldn't name what it was or what was missing and why they were treating each other like this.

◆ ◆ ◆

On Goran's last day in Rio, Katia took him to see the favela where her mother lived. After visiting Dona Ana, they were on their way back down the steep pathway from the higher part of the favela where Ana lived when Katia saw a young woman she had met on one of her earlier visits. The woman smiled at Katia and looked at Goran.

Ele é seu namorado? "Is he your boyfriend?"

Katia smiled.

Ele é gringo? "Is he a foreigner?"

Ele é gringo, Katia responded.

Ele é bonito, the woman said. "He's handsome."

"He is, isn't he?" Katia said in Portuguese, smiling at the woman. Katia reached for Goran's hand. He gave a slight smile but he did not ask Katia to translate. They continued walking.

"What were you saying back there? That I'm a *gringo*?"

"Yeah. But it doesn't mean the same here. That's just what they call all foreigners."

"*They* called me a gringo, or *you* called me a gringo?" he said, his voice becoming tense.

"Goran, what does it matter? You're a gringo to them ..."

"Don't fucking call me a gringo. And I'd appreciate if you didn't let them call me that."

"It's not anything negative, alright? It's not like in Mexico or the rest of Latin America. It's just the term for a foreigner, a European or American or Argentinean or whoever. Why are you making such a big ..."

"And you're *not* one?"

"No, well I mean yes, but I'm also from here. My birth family is from here so no, I guess I'm not completely gringo."

She looked at him.

"Goran, why this attitude?"

"Because I feel like a fucking appendage here."

They reached the plaza at the base of the favela.

"I want to go for a walk on the beach. Let's get a taxi," she said.

They were silent in the car. The taxi driver asked where they were from.

"*Americanos*," she said. "Well, he's from Bosnia originally but grew up in the US and I was born in Rio de Janeiro and live in the US also."

The taxi driver, a man in his early sixties, looked back at her from the rear view mirror.

"You're a Carioca then," he said in Portuguese, with a jovial smile. "*Mas ele é gringo.*"

Katia smiled back at the taxi driver, and did not translate for Goran. She hoped Goran was not paying attention. She looked out the window while Goran continued glowering for the rest of the taxi ride.

The sun had begun to set as they walked along the beach in silence. They were not holding hands. They walked on the sidewalk, with the alternating grey and black tiles. Occasionally she felt the light abrasiveness of sand under her shoes.

They walked in the direction of Dois Irmaõs, the mountain peaks at the end of Leblon, with the ocean to their left and the mountain in front of them, the favela climbing up its side. There were scattered sunbathers. In the distance, they could see surfers taking advantage of the large waves.

"I wrote to her," he finally said.

"I knew you would. Good for you."

"I just wrote her, okay? I wanted to tell you, that's all. I told her it would be nice to catch up, to know what she's up to, what happened to her. I found out she's working for an NGO that ..."

"It's okay," she said. "I don't need to know any more. You don't owe me any explanation."

"I know I don't. I wanted to share that with you."

They turned to walk in the direction of her apartment and continued in silence. When they arrived, she stayed in the living room while he finished packing. He took a long shower while she wrote emails and looked at Facebook.

His bag packed, he moved his things close to the front door and opened his laptop. For a few minutes, the only sound in the apartment was the clicking of their keyboards mixed with the muffled sounds of cars from the street. She offered to make him something to eat before he traveled but he declined.

When the intercom rang to announce that the taxi had arrived, it startled them. He insisted that she didn't need to see him off at the airport. She didn't insist on going along. She walked him downstairs.

"Katia, I'm sorry. I didn't want to leave it like …"

"Goran, it's okay. Or it's not okay. We'll talk more when I'm back."

She continued, "Thank you for coming. It meant a lot."

"Good luck on your trip to Bahia."

She nodded and he got into the taxi. They kissed quickly.

For the first time, Katia found herself assessing and grading. She had moved in with Goran and started whatever this was with him with no checklist in mind. She despised that dating-website logic of some of her female friends. But now, as she weighed it all up, she found she wasn't so sure.

MUSEUM SUBMISSION 27-2011

He was a fellow seminarian with a room two doors down from mine. He helped carry my bags the day I arrived, then explained the routines, and introduced me around.

When he asked, I told him about my family in Mexico and why I wanted to be a priest. Part of the reason was faith. And part of the reason was that it gave me the opportunity to travel and to study, things my family never had the money for me to do. If he judged me for this, he didn't show it.

Later, he showed me pictures of his family. I could tell they were wealthy. He said they would never accept who he really was. I wasn't sure what he meant.

He came in one night just a few weeks after I had arrived. He knocked, then he opened the door part of the way and said my name. Whatever I said must have sounded inviting. He told me he had enjoyed talking to me and then I reached out to touch him. That was the first of many nights.

The end of my second month there, he decided to leave. Said he wasn't cut out for the priesthood. Said he needed to live the kind of love and desire he felt. That he couldn't lead a double life. I laughed and asked him who it was he was having sex with when he came to my room.

I told him I could love him and become a priest.

He said that I didn't really love him, that I was just having sex with a man for the first time.

He knew that his words hurt, even if he was right. I don't think he meant them to sound as harsh as they did. He just told me everything that came into his head. I wonder if that isn't love. To be able to tell someone everything you think.

He left me this rosary. I couldn't touch it without thinking of his hands on me.

I see his pictures on Facebook now and then. He has a husband. They have a dog and a yard.

I've learned to live with the guilt. We have a sacrament for that. It's missing him that I haven't learned how to live with.

Boston, USA, 2011

Tyler

One warm Saturday night a few weeks later, Tyler and Carla and the boys drove the thirty-five minutes into Austin and had dinner on the outdoor patio of a barbecue restaurant that had live music. Here, far enough from the apartment complex, they were affectionate with each other in front of the boys.

After they ate, Tyler carried the boys back to the car, both laughing and running their hands through his hair.

"Are you my mommy's boyfriend?" Joaquin said as Tyler put him down next to the car.

Tyler looked in Carla's direction, seeking a cue. He saw the slight smile on her face.

"Yes, I suppose I am," Tyler said. "Is that okay with you?"

Joaquin shrugged his shoulders. "I guess so," he said.

Tyler looked over and saw Sammy listening attentively. "Okay with you too, buddy?" Tyler asked.

"Yeah," he said.

◆ ◆ ◆

"Do you think Mommy's getting better?" Sammy asked Tyler later that same week.

Sammy showed Tyler a picture of her that he had drawn.

"What's that?" Tyler asked pointing to a square image in the drawing.

"That's Mommy in a hospital."

Sammy's drawing showed a building and a lopsided car that was apparently an ambulance.

"I'm sure she's fine. You know she loves you. Just sometimes big people have problems they need to work on. But it has nothing to do with you. And that's why we have two parents, so the other one can take care of you and love you too."

"She said she was sick."

Tyler stared at the drawing.

"Did she say what was the matter?"

Sammy shook his head.

"Did you ever see her sick?"

Sammy shrugged his shoulders.

"She just got all sad sometimes. She said that her head hurt real deep inside."

"I'm glad she brought you to stay with me. That was the best thing to do so she can focus on getting better."

Tyler was using some of the sentences his therapist suggested.

"Yeah," Sammy said. "I guess so. We get to do boy stuff."

"Yeah," Tyler said.

Tyler would have pondered it more, about what might have motivated Melissa, about what was causing her headaches and the sadness that Sammy described. About where she had gone all those times when she used to disappear during the months they were together as a couple. About how she could have cut herself off from Sammy like that and convinced her friends and family to go along with it. But it was easier to focus on Sammy, and on his own urgent desire to spend every moment with Carla.

◆ ◆ ◆

Later that same week, Tyler and Sammy went over to
Carla and Joaquin's apartment for dinner. Tyler and
Carla sat at the dining table after washing the dishes.

"Are you okay?" Tyler asked.

"He called today."

"Your ex?"

"Yeah."

"He knows he has a restraining order and that he can't
call you or come near you, right?"

"Yeah, he knows."

"What did he want?"

"He said he wants to talk, that he wants to do right by
Joaquin."

"What did you tell him?"

"I reminded him that he can't call me and that these
are things that will be discussed in court."

"What did he say?"

"He said 'why can't we just work this out without law-
yers and shit?' He said he knows he hurt me and he
knows there's no going back but he wants to work it out
for Joaquin. I told him it was too late for that and that it
could be worse for him if he tried calling me again. Then
he said my name, soft like. Then he hung up."

"Are you okay?"

"Yeah, I think so."

"What?"

"I'm just worried about what he might do if he found
out about us. I mean I don't think that he'd ..."

"That's why I'm here and that's why you have a restraining order. It'll be okay," he said and held her.

"I just want it to stay like this, between you and me."

"I know, so do I."

He looked over her shoulder in the direction of the living room, watching the two boys, their bodies at nearly identical angles, their unblinking eyes glued to the movie on the TV. He knew he should leave right then, pick up Sammy and go. Ask to be reassigned, report the phone call from her ex, tell Carla he could see her but only away from here, and only after some time had passed.

Instead he held her close to him and nuzzled his nose in her neck and smelled her hair.

◆ ◆ ◆

A few days later, as Tyler came back to the apartment complex, he noticed a truck parked on the street with a man sitting inside. Through his aviator shades Tyler could tell that the man was looking in the direction of the apartment complex. He saw the man's eyes and brow, unmistakably the same as Joaquin's.

Tyler parked on the street outside the apartment complex and walked over to the truck. The man turned toward Tyler, showing no apparent concern. The man's look suggested he was expecting Tyler to come over.

"Afternoon," Tyler said, approaching the driver's side of the truck.

"Afternoon," the man said.

He could have been of Italian descent, or Hispanic, solidly built, with dark hair, a fierce nose and dark eyebrows.

"I'm with the Bastrop Sheriff's Department."

"No shit."

"Do you live around here or have some business around here?"

"Anything wrong with parking here?"

"Depends on who you are and if you have a restraining order."

The man stared hard at him, then said, "That would be a problem, I guess."

"You're Carla Salazar's ex."

"Yup. Name is Steven. In case you wanted to know."

"You know you can't be here. And you know I could arrest you."

"So you're their rent-a-cop. That's convenient."

Tyler rested his hand on the top of the truck.

"You need to leave. You know the rules."

"But you get to be here."

Tyler looked out onto the street and then back at Steven.

"You a vet?" Steven asked.

"Yeah. Afghanistan," Tyler eventually said.

"I was in Iraq *and* Afghanistan. You lose your woman when you went over? Or did she wait for you?"

Tyler paused, before saying: "We broke up before I left. Then I came back and she left me with a son. One I didn't know I had. And then she took off. Never came back."

"Yeah, well, mine left me and took the kid with her. At least you got the kid."

"You can get supervised visits. That is if you obey the restraining order and anything else the court mandates."

"But supervised visits aren't quite the same as you being with them, is it? Hanging with them whenever you want."

"You know the rules. And if you break them, it'll make it worse for you and for them."

"You see combat in Afghanistan? Shoot at Taliban?"

Tyler hesitated, thinking he should find a way to end the conversation.

"I was in combat. But no, I never fired on them."

"Where were you?"

"Kandahar."

"You were in Kandahar and you never fired at Taliban? Lose your weapon or something?"

"I knew where my weapon was all the time. And I know where it is now."

Steven stared at him; his glare was aggressive. Then Steven nodded and curled his lip slightly into his mouth. He looked at Tyler just long enough for it to be uncomfortable.

"Tell me something. You keep your gun on you when you're banging her? You think I don't know what's going on between you two? Now I get it. Your woman leaves you and you take up with another guy's wife. And you're supposed to be the cop who watches over them."

Tyler paused before responding. He didn't know if Steven was making wild guesses or if Carla may have said something. He had seen fellow soldiers break down when they got *Dear John* letters or, worse, when they heard from third parties that their girlfriends or wives had hooked up with someone else. He thought it safest to lean toward honesty.

"Your story with Carla and mine have nothing to do with each other," Tyler said.

"So, just like that, she's yours, huh? Convenient, isn't it? Right next door. You having a right to be here and all. Their protector."

"It's time you left," Tyler said. He moved his hand to his waist. For a moment he thought about the gun that was resting in its holder inside the backpack he had left in his car.

"I wonder if your bosses would find it interesting to know that the cop they assigned to the shelter was screwing one of the women he's supposed to be protecting."

"If you don't leave right now, they'll take my word that you violated your restraining order. I don't think they'll care much about anything else."

"You keep screwing my wife and I may have to make a call to the Bastrop sheriff's department."

Steven started his truck and Tyler took a half step away from it. He hated domestic violence cases. Tyler always hoped it was other police officers who had to arrest the men.

MUSEUM SUBMISSION 11-2010

My wife and I were so happy the day we were married. We had a love marriage. Our families were not pleased about that.

I didn't have a job and my father said they had no room for us. My wife offered to work in the tea estate to pay for rent. I know how hard that is. So I got work at a tea shop in town and we moved into a very small apartment.

Our first child was a boy and then we had a second one. When our boys started school, there were fees to pay and books and uniforms to buy. The shop I worked in was bought by another man. He had his own workers.

My wife decided to go abroad for work, like many women here do. It is easy to find the recruiters and easy to get the visa. She was in Kuwait for seven years. Every month she wired us money and I paid the rent and the school fees. With the little that was left over, I saved until finally I was able to build a house.

The boys were happy when we moved in. They drew pictures of the house for their mother and I mailed them to her.

Our hearts were filled with joy when she came back.

But the woman I married is not the same woman who came back to us. This is the picture of us after we got married. See how happy she looks. How full of life she is. Her voice is the same. I can see in her face the woman I fell in love with. But it is not her.

She does not laugh like she used to. She watches the boys and is happy to be with them. She cares for the house I built. But she looks at it as if it is not hers. As if this is not really her life.

Late at night when I am awake and the house is quiet I think that somewhere over there in Kuwait, in that land filled with oil and sheiks and camels and big air-conditioned malls that stretch for kilometers, my real wife is sleeping, or perhaps waking up, with a smile like the one she has in this picture on the day we were married.

Kandy, Sri Lanka, 2011

Katia

A few days after Goran returned to Chicago, Katia approached Felipe as they walked out of Portuguese class.

"Are you going to yoga today?"

"Yeah."

"Can I have a ride? I mean if that's okay."

"Sure."

They were silent on the way there.

When the yoga class was over, they again walked out together.

"You want to get a beer?" Felipe asked. "*Aquele chope?*"

"Yes," she said, smiling. "I would like that very much."

He was a funny lover, eager to please one moment, self-absorbed the next. Katia tried not to compare him to Goran, or to other American guys she had been with. Still, she could not avoid remembering what one of the English women in her Portuguese classes had told her about her Carioca lover. That he was enjoyable in bed but lazy. Katia thought she knew what the woman meant.

The next morning she noticed the wall in his bedroom. There were photos of Felipe and of friends, and dozens of pictures of the same woman, dark-haired with rounded, girlish cheeks and perfect, long straight hair. There were phrases, mostly place names, written on post-it notes next to the pictures. The handwriting was neater and more flamboyant than the way he wrote on the white-board during Portuguese class.

Katia stood naked in front of the pictures after she came back from the bathroom.

"Who is she?" she asked. "Just curious."

"That's Andrea. She was my girlfriend for my last year at university and after that. Still is, I guess."

His voice had the same light-hearted tone he usually did.

"So you guys are together?"

"She's doing her master's in the UK. She'll be there at least two years. We left it open. We thought it was going to be impossible to wait that long. She'll probably come back for a visit either at the end of her summer or maybe Christmas, but that's it. She'll travel in Europe. If I can afford it, I'll meet her there for a few weeks. But we left it open, you know, about seeing other people."

Katia controlled herself; she wanted to ask more. *Do you love her? Do you love her in that way that it feels like you're empty without her? Does she make you forget everything else? Do you imagine being with her twenty years from now? Does something feel ripped out of you when you think you may lose her?*

Katia sat on the end of the bed, facing the photos and arching her back. Felipe moved one of his feet up her back slowly and then along the side of her thigh. Then he sat up and moved toward her crossing his arms around her. As he held her, Katia looked at the smile on Andrea's face in the photos. She thought about Goran. Felipe didn't ask if they had broken up or how the visit had gone. He hadn't asked about Goran at all. Nor had she volunteered anything.

She opened her legs and he understood what she wanted. As she trembled she knew she wanted Felipe to go with her on the trip to Bahia. And she thought that Felipe might be a quick learner after all.

◆ ◆ ◆

"Did they tell you anything more about your real mother?"

Felipe and Katia were waiting in Rio airport for their flight to Salvador, Bahia.

"My adoptive mother worked at an NGO that had projects in Santa Marta. That's how she knew about her and about what happened to her. They showed me a newspaper article that had a picture of my biological mother. And my mother, I mean my adoptive mother, had a CD with this song that she said my biological mother sang to me before she was killed. It goes like this ..."

Katia hummed a slow melody.

"That was about the only thing I knew about my biological mother all these years."

Felipe nodded and then translated the words for her.

On this street, on this street there is a forest called loneliness
And there lives the angel that stole my heart
If I stole, oh if I stole your heart, you stole mine too
And if I stole your heart it's because I love you true
If this street were mine, oh if it were mine
I would make them pave it with tiny diamonds, tiny diamonds
Just to watch you pass by, just to watch you pass by.

"It's called *Se essa rua fosse minha*. If this street were mine," Felipe said.

She reached for his hand.

"I think my nanny sang it to me, too," he continued. "I think every nanny or mother in Brazil sings it."

At the Salvador airport they rented a car and made the three-hour drive westward, leaving the tropical vegetation of the coast and entering the increasingly dry *sertão*, the desert plains of Brazil's northeast.

Katia's grandmother lived about forty minutes by car outside a small town called Retirolandia. They stopped for lunch in the town square. It was a one-block by one-block square filled with jacaranda trees, their red flowers giving off the only color of any significance. The base of each tree was painted white from the ground to about one meter up. There were a few open-air restaurants around the square, all covered with the same terracotta roof tiles. They chose one and Felipe ordered goat kebobs and beers.

When their dishes came, they smiled at how chewy the goat meat was as they both struggled to pull it off the skewers. Katia was quiet and Felipe filled in the silence by explaining that in this part of Bahia they planted sugar cane and *sisal*, the straw used to make handbags and hats.

"Both are pretty horrible. What with the heat when you're in the fields and the plants cutting into your hands."

Katia nodded, but they both knew she was not really paying attention.

After lunch they drove along a narrow road through sugarcane plantations and small farms. The houses on the farms were made of mud and stucco walls and corrugated zinc or tile roofs. Except for the power lines, nothing around them looked to be have been built in the past fifty years. They came to the turn-off that led to her grandmother's house.

Katia looked at the house and opened the car door. There were goats grazing on the sparse vegetation. Some of them raised their heads and regarded Katia and Felipe. She took a deep breath and inhaled the slight odor of animals and the fermenting refuse of sugar cane. She looked at Felipe and he reached for her hand. She took a deep breath to steady herself.

As they stepped out of the car, Felipe followed about two steps behind her. They walked toward the door of the house, which had a thin cloth acting as a screen. Katia stood a step away from the door and called out.

"*Dona Lidia. Esta em casa?*" she said, attempting to repeat the same cadence she had heard the pastor use when they went to visit her great aunt Ana in the favela in Rio. She hoped Lidia would be expecting her. Felipe had helped Katia make a call a week before and it seemed Lidia was excited that her American granddaughter would be coming to visit.

Katia waved a fly off her face. From inside the house she heard movement and shuffling across the floor. Through the hanging cloth she could make out the shape of a woman who walked with some difficulty. The woman moved the cloth aside and stepped outside to greet them.

The woman was wearing a flower-print skirt and an untucked, loose-fitting, sleeveless blouse. Her long afro had a few gray hairs and was tied back with a white cloth. Katia thought that her grandmother looked older than she must have been. She waited for her grandmother to speak first.

Her grandmother carried out an inspection of her, as if trying to confirm that Katia was indeed her granddaughter.

"*Minha filha. Minha neta. Minha querida. Voce esta aqui*

depois de todos estes anos." My child. My granddaughter. My darling. You're here after all these years.

Her grandmother spoke slowly. Katia didn't know if this was her normal way of speaking or if she was overwhelmed by this moment.

"Avô," Katia said. *Grandmother.*

They hugged and Katia felt her grandmother's skin against hers, the looser skin of her grandmother's arms engulfing her own. Her grandmother pulled away and looked Katia in the eyes again. She began to cry as she looked at Katia and held Katia's face in her hands.

"*Não vou chorar mais. Ja chorei demais todos estes anos,*" her grandmother said, taking her hands off Katia's face and wiping her own eyes with the end of her skirt. *I won't cry anymore. I've already cried too much all these years.*

Without saying anything else, her grandmother invited them inside and then excused herself and stepped out of the room.

While she was gone, Katia looked around. She regarded the cement floor, the calendar from a pharmacy hanging on the wall, the wooden cross hanging next to it, the flies that flitted on and off the small coffee table. She had imagined it would be like this but seeing it left her feeling partly guilty and partly out of place.

Katia heard the goats outside and was hit by a pungent smell from the kitchen, which she thought might have been from soured goat milk. Another cloth hung in the doorway that led to the kitchen and the bedroom. Katia wanted to let herself in, to see the kitchen, or to be invited into the inner circle of the house.

Her grandmother came back a few minutes later carrying a wooden tray with coffee and water. Behind her was a slightly younger woman.

"This is my cousin, Cida. She lives here too. Helps me

take care of the goats. A widow like me," her grand-mother said.

Katia stood up to greet Cida, who smiled and reached out to hold Katia's arm.

"You do look just like her," Cida said, still holding on to Katia's arm. "I just wanted to see you, child. I'll let you carry on."

Cida nodded at Felipe as she stepped out.

"And this young man?" her grandmother said. "He must be the friend you talked about?"

"I'm Felipe. It's a pleasure to meet you Dona Lidia."

"*Homem bonito,*" Lidia said, looking at Katia and taking Felipe's hand with both of hers.

As she finished pouring coffee, Lidia began telling the story of Katia's mother. Katia turned to Felipe when she needed help translating. The words flowed onto her, over her, slowly penetrating her. Her grandmother repeated parts that Katia already knew, about how her biological parents met, about the gangs, about the wedding.

Then Lidia told the rest, the part she had not heard before.

"Nobody prepares a mother to have her daughter treated like an x9. Nobody. Nobody deserves that. No mother deserves that."

Katia turned to Felipe and with her eyes signaled that she wanted him to translate.

"x9 is an informer," he said. "A traitor. Someone who gives information on the gang to the police or a rival gang. They usually execute them."

Her grandmother turned away, struggling to keep from crying.

"Did you understand?" Felipe asked.

Katia heard the words *lit on fire*, *wedding*, and *dress* but they all ran together. From her father's research in Brazil, Katia had heard the stories of the various forms of execution that the drug gangs in Rio de Janeiro carried out. But it had never seemed real to her. It was just harsh images from his work and from a life far away.

"She lived for a time. She was strong. Our kind don't die easily."

Lidia paused and then said, "I have something for you," and left the room again.

Her grandmother came back two minutes later with a small *figa*, a hand with the thumb crossed through the middle and index fingers, a good luck charm, part of Brazil's African traditions, supposed to ward off evil spirits and bad luck.

"I used to think that this didn't work," Lidia said, holding it in one hand. "My Fatima died. And nothing could stop them from killing her. But then I thought that it was for you, not for her. It worked for *you*. You were born. She lived just long enough to have you and to see you. She had you and then died a few days later. You should have this."

Felipe explained what it was and Katia nodded. It was made of onyx and was on a thin silver chain. Katia ran her fingers over it and then closed her palm around it.

"Your mother sang a song to you," Lidia continued. "I heard her singing it to you once before she died. I should have stayed by her side those last days before she passed away but I was so angry at her and how she took up with your father and what he did. I could hardly stand it. I knew from the beginning that nothing good would come of him. I couldn't bear looking at her after what he did. I never imagined they would kill her. What mother can imagine that for their child?"

Then her grandmother sang a few lines of the song. Her grandmother sang it as Katia imagined that her own mother must have sung it to her.

On this street, on this street there is a forest called
loneliness
And there lives the angel that stole my heart
If I stole, oh if I stole your heart, you stole mine too …

"Well, now you know," Lidia said. "Now you know it all."

Sang by her grandmother, the lines were was as plaintive and arid as the land around them. Katia let her tears run. Lidia held her hands as Katia finally understood how her birth mother was killed and why Kevin and her mother could not have told her this.

Felipe walked over to Katia and put a hand on her shoulder as she continued to cry. Katia turned to him and let him embrace her.

"You understand why I couldn't stay in Rio," Lidia said. "And in Santa Marta. I couldn't see those people again. I couldn't bear to live in the place where that had happened."

Katia nodded.

"It was better that you went to the States. There was nothing for you here, *minha filha*. It was the best thing I ever did. I never met the woman who adopted you but I heard she was a good person. I'm sure she's been good to you. If I were twenty years younger I'd ask you to take me with you. Imagine me trying to learn English, now. There's nothing for you here, *minha filha*."

Katia nodded again.

"I want to stay in touch. I can come back. Maybe …"

Her grandmother reached over and patted Katia's hands to hush her.

"I'm so glad you came. I'm so glad I got to see you all grown up. *Minha querida neta* Katia."

Lidia stared at her. Katia wondered for a moment why her grandmother didn't ask more about her, what she did, if she was in love with Felipe, or with someone else, or who he was and what he was to her, what it was like growing up in the US, what her adoptive parents were like.

Felipe excused himself, saying he was going to walk around outside. Katia and her grandmother watched him leave and then looked at each other again, holding hands and nodding slightly.

"Minha linda neta. Diretamente dos Estados Unidos."

Lidia ran her hands over Katia's shoulders, feeling the cloth of her colorful blouse and touching Katia's polished silver hoop earrings, then holding Katia's cheeks. Katia couldn't tell if it was her youth or her health that her grandmother was admiring, or if it was what her clothes said about how far Katia had gone from all of this.

"I have something else for you," Lidia said and got up. Katia watched the difficulty of her movements, and the slowness in her grandmother's step. Her grandmother opened a small notebook that lay next to the television and pulled out a weathered color photo and handed it to Katia. Then she opened a drawer in a stand by the TV and pulled out what looked like a clothing box. There were yellowed stains on the otherwise white cardboard box.

"This is your mother, just before all that happened. And the box is for you to open later, when you're ready."

Katia looked at the photo of a girl, a teenager, her hair straightened, wearing a skin-tight halter top and jeans shorts. It was as if she were looking at a slight variation of herself at that age. She rested her hands on the top of the box.

"You keep them. Take them with you."

Katia waited for her grandmother to say more. She expected more stories, or perhaps an invitation to stay for dinner, or for her grandmother to show her around the small farm, to explain how they raised the goats and to tell her the names each of the plants in the garden.

"I'm so glad I got to see you all grown up," Lidia said.

"I'm glad I met you," Katia said.

Her grandmother stood up and hugged Katia briefly.

"Give a hug to Ana before you leave Brazil."

Lidia walked Katia outside. Felipe, who had been leaning against the car, walked toward them and gave Lidia a goodbye kiss on each cheek.

As Felipe started the car, Katia was grateful that he closed the windows and turned on the air conditioning.

They were mostly silent on the four-hour drive back to Salvador. Felipe plugged his phone into the USB jack in the rental car and put on a playlist of the singer Marissa Monte. A singer he remembered Katia had said she liked in class.

It was nearly 9 p.m. when they arrived in Salvador. Katia was pleased to feel the humidity when she opened the car door as they parked in the lot behind the hotel they had reserved in the old colonial part of the city. They checked in, left their bags in the small room filled with simple period pieces, and then sat in the cobblestone square outside the hotel for a drink. Felipe glanced at the messages on his phone.

The hotel was across from one of the white, opulent colonial churches. Katia was glad that the low light coming from the few street lamps allowed her to fade into the shadows. In the distance she could hear a drumbeat. She couldn't tell if it was live or coming from a nearby night club.

"Do you want to walk around and see the old town?" Felipe asked, after they finished their drinks.

"Let's go to the room," she said.

"Ok," he said and followed her.

She reached for his hand as they climbed the stairs to their floor. Smiling at him when they got into the room, Katia undressed and motioned for him to follow her into the shower. They were still partly wet when they threw off their towels and fell onto the bed. As she closed her eyes and came, she was glad that Felipe couldn't tell that her mind was far away.

MUSEUM SUBMISSION 23-2010

After two years together we decided to have a child. Her sister had two children and we adored being aunt and uncle. For nearly three years we tried to get pregnant. Finally the doctors said the only way we could conceive was in vitro.

I remember the first time I masturbated in the tiny room at the fertility clinic. Here was my wish to have a child in this plastic container that looked like the kind used for stool samples. I walked out of the room and took the flask to the male nurse. He smiled like he was trying to make it all seem normal.

Finally it worked. The doctor was pleased when she showed us the results. We were both happy.

We made plans. We moved to a bigger place and prepared the baby's room. Some weekends we went to my parents' beach house and spent hours talking about all that we would do once our baby was born.

In between all of that, I had a lover. She was a doctoral student at the university where I taught. A baby was the last thing I wanted with her. But she decided to keep the child. She asked me to come to the clinic with her to a prenatal visit. I told her I didn't want to be involved with the child but I went with her to the clinic. She drove us there and I was so distracted that it wasn't until we were walking inside that I realized it was the same clinic my wife and I came to.

Less than a week later I was back at the clinic with my wife. It was the same receptionist on duty from the week before. She looked at me for a long while and then asked me, weren't you here last week? My wife responded that it had been six weeks since our last visit. The receptionist said that she was sure she had just seen me.

My wife stared at me.

I stared back at the receptionist. I tried to explain to my wife how I felt masturbating into that flask. That I didn't mean to hurt her. That makes it worse, doesn't it? Of all the stupid things to say. Still I said it: *I didn't mean to hurt you.*

My wife cried as we sat in the car in the parking lot at the clinic. She told me she expected me to do my half and that we could have joint custody. She stopped crying and asked me to drive her to our apartment. She waited while I packed my things.

Here's one of those flasks they use at the clinic. And here is the book I was going to give my wife the day our child was born, an original edition of Neruda's love poems that I found at a flea market after we found out we were going to have a baby.

Santiago, Chile, 2010

Goran

The day before Goran traveled to Brazil to see Katia and go with her to the favela where her mother had been raised, he wrote a postcard to Nikoleta. He tore up his first two attempts. Finally, satisfied with the message he had composed, he mailed it to the museum. He didn't know where the postcard would be forwarded to— whether Nikoleta lived in Canada, Bosnia, or somewhere else in the Balkans these days. But he was convinced it would reach her.

He had been home from his trip to Brazil for two days, still brooding about how it had ended, when he received an email with a subject line that said: "Your postcard."

My dearest Goran. It is lovely to hear from you after all this time. I never imagined you'd see the letter I sent to the museum. Just kind of a funny thing I decided to do after I visited it a year ago. I figured I had a story that belonged there.

It would be nice to see you. As it happens, I will be in Mostar for the second half of the summer. If you get this message, and want to meet up, send me a text and we can try to find a time, if you haven't already returned to Chicago. Warm wishes, Nikoleta

Goran didn't immediately respond. Some years before, he had done a Google search of her name and found the website of the organization where she worked. He had read articles she had written. He remembered finding one low-resolution picture of her on a blog. She was standing among a group of women, posing for one of those staff retreat photos. All he could see clearly was that her hair was still long and reddish-brown, and her smile was still irreverent. Now, he Googled her again and found her name was still there. This time there was no picture of her.

Finally he responded, asking how long she would be in Mostar. Katia was still in Brazil and Goran had six weeks before classes resumed at the university where he taught in Chicago. He looked at flights online, and even though he had wiped out most of his savings account with the previous two trips of the summer, he booked it.

Goran responded to Nikoleta that he would be back in Sarajevo in three weeks. They could meet in Mostar as she suggested. She responded the next day saying she would be happy to see him.

◆ ◆ ◆

Three weeks later Goran rented a car at Sarajevo airport and began the drive to Mostar, passing through forests and by rivers, with occasional views of snow-capped mountains. Even though he wasn't really hungry, he stopped at a restaurant with lamb roasting on open spits outside—one that had been there since he was a kid, and that had re-opened after the war.

When he arrived in Mostar, he found a small hotel near the old part of town; the hotel's exterior was made of the same pale limestone that was used for the medieval buildings nearby. He dropped his bag in the room and went for a walk.

Goran had not yet told Nikoleta he had arrived. Nor

had he texted Katia to tell her his exact travel dates. After returning from Brazil, he had texted her just once asking how the trip to visit her grandmother went, and telling her that he planned to spend some time in Bosnia before the summer ended. Katia responded with a text saying: *I'm glad you're going. It's important. It was important for me to go to Bahia. Lots to talk about when we meet again. Tell me when you'll be back.*

Goran wanted to spend at least a few hours in Bosnia on his own, maybe longer, to be Yugoslavian or Bosnian or Serbian or whatever he was again without feeling like a tour guide. He hadn't planned it, but he realized that neither Katia, nor his mother, nor Nikoleta, nor his father, nor any of his friends knew exactly where he was. This solitude grounded him.

He walked for nearly two hours with no destination, turning randomly and walking through parks and side streets, in modern parts of the city as well as the old town. Finally, he stopped at a café by the river in the old city. In one direction, bright green vegetation covered the river banks and, above the river, there were medieval stone buildings and a solitary minaret in the same mottled, beige stone color. Beyond that there were hills with patches of green. On the other side of him he saw the infamous bridge, the one destroyed in the war and then rebuilt with its magnificent arch, and its nearly identical fortress-like buildings on each side.

He texted Nikoleta. When his phone chimed with a text message from her a few minutes later, he felt a wave of anticipation. She suggested they meet at the bridge in an hour. He finished another coffee, opened his book, then asked for a shot of rakija. An hour later, he hadn't turned a single page.

◆ ◆ ◆

They had not specified on which side of the bridge they would meet. As he turned to lean against the wall on one side of the bridge, he saw her. Nikoleta had not seen him yet. She was looking at the ground as she walked. At first he thought she was wearing high heels and was struggling with the uneven stone pavement. Then he thought she had twisted her ankle. She was wearing black leggings and a tunic-style, long blouse that clung to her hips; he followed the line of the blouse down her leg expecting to see a cast on her foot.

All he could tell was that her walk was irregular; it looked painful and he forced himself to smile until she looked up at him. He felt like rushing toward her and helping her, but knew instinctively that he had to wait for her where he was. As she got closer, he saw that she had a cane in one hand.

"Hey," he said as she reached him.

"Hey," she said, matching his smile.

They took a moment just looking at each other.

He moved a step toward her and leaned into her to kiss her on the cheek and she steadied herself against the wall. Her hair blew in the breeze and she shielded her eyes from the afternoon sun.

"Goran. My dearest Goran. You're really here."

"Nikoleta, it's so good to see you," he said. "I still can't believe I found your letter. Yeah, well, and now I'm here."

He could not tell what he saw in her eyes. He couldn't read if it was happiness, confusion, anger, scorn, or maybe all of those things.

"Let's walk, shall we? I've been in meetings all day."

He looked at her briefly, surprised that she would suggest this.

"Of course," he said.

She had rested her cane against the wall and he watched her reach for it. Her moves were automatic, adjusting for the cane, and moving her weight to accommodate whatever damage had been done to her hip or leg. As she started moving, her gait told of bones broken or twisted. He tried to connect this version of her with the girl he had watched running for cover from the rain in the transit camp.

It required effort not to stare at her as she walked; he made himself look straight ahead.

"So, what are you doing in Mostar? Tell me about your job, how your work is going, and ...," he started.

She looked at him.

"Goran, do you really want to start with that? Of course we can. But it's been nearly twenty years since we met and ... that's what Americans always ask. *What do you do?* Have you become *that* American?"

He looked over at her for a moment and nodded.

"Ok."

He paused, then restarted. His words came with a slow and uneven pace that nearly matched her walk.

"Yeah, okay, so where to start. Shit, for years I thought about finding you," he said, not looking at her. "I think that kept me sane, you know, when I was trying to be something like a normal teenager in Chicago. Being an immigrant and all that."

"I imagined you there. I hoped you found your American life. It wasn't easy here. I guess you know that. But maybe you don't know how hard it was to stay safe during that time."

He continued, not really hearing the meaning of her words.

"I never really stopped thinking about you, you know,

wondering what happened," he said.

Now he turned to look at her, trying to judge if he should continue, if this was a waste of emotional energy, if he sounded ridiculous, if she could sense his anxiety.

"Until I met Katia, my girlfriend, and I kind of stopped thinking about you for a while. Then I saw your letter in the museum. I was with her when I saw it. I obviously hadn't expected that. She saw it too. And the way I reacted to it. That kind of threw things up in the air between us. I mean it makes no sense but ..."

Goran wondered if Nikoleta thought about it too: the first time they had met twenty years before. Back then he had also been nervous and it had seemed to him then, as now, that she was the one in charge.

Nikoleta smiled. It was a smile he recognized. Then she gave a little laugh, a proud laugh. He wasn't sure what she meant by it. He no longer trusted his ability to read Yugoslavian irony.

"That letter was a little melodramatic, don't you think?" she said. "But it's a good story. The people at the museum told me it gets lots of comments."

He walked, and she continued her halting gait, her head going up and down as if she were an old pull-toy on a hinge that bobbed as it advanced. They brushed hips at one point and he moved away quickly, afraid he would topple her.

"Don't tell me you left your girlfriend waiting ... for me," she said, the last word corresponding with the apex of the arc of her head-bobbing limp. "Will she take you back knowing you've come to chase your teenage past and found this?" she said, looking down at her cane.

He wanted to ask her what had happened to her, why she limped.

"And you, you don't limp. You seem to be intact, all

your limbs. No sports injuries. No war injuries. You came out okay, it seems. You got out of here just in time."

"I guess. It was hard without my father. He never joined us after we left. I've seen him just once since then and that was, well … He has a new family I've never even met."

"Ah, yes, that's right. He stayed behind when your mother and you and your brother left."

"Does that count?" he said.

"Divorced parents? An absent father? I don't think so. That's half of humanity."

He smiled.

"You're thinking something," she said. "You're not telling me. You're afraid of what I'll say, aren't you?"

"Maybe," he said.

He looked at her, trying to get used to her.

"I think I talked to you in my head all these years. Or at least I imagined we'd find each other again and then I rehearsed what I would tell you when we eventually met," he said.

She smiled, an ironic smile. "It's easier if you say things out loud. Or write me. You could have tried that. Internet, you know about that? You could have found me."

He tried to ignore the bitterness.

"I was thinking that what I lost in the war was you or someone like you. My wound is missing you—this girl I talked to in my head. Obsessing over you, really. I mean, even if we had had time together and then broken up and moved on with the rest of our lives, which is probably what would have happened, that moment was lost. Taken from us."

She was silent.

"Sure, that counts," she said. "You might be able to go

to the international tribunal in The Hague with that one. Almost the same as living through a war."

She gave him a look that made him turn away.

"It was a lifetime ago, wasn't it? We've had lives since then, grown-up lives. Things have happened to us. You had your teenage years in Chicago and I was here, trying to survive. It was just that, those two days when we were, what, fourteen, fifteen? What worried me about finding you was that we'd try to make it into something it isn't or wasn't. Like if we found each other we could erase a war and everything that happened."

He turned back to look at her.

"I suppose we had something real in that transit camp. As real as anything is when you're fifteen years old. It was serious. At the same time, how could we live believing we'd find each other one day? We're Yugoslavians— well, not even that anymore. We're Bosnians and we know better. Do you even call yourself a Bosnian these days?"

As she said this, she turned to him and he could feel a provocation in her eyes. He did not respond.

"I'm not a girl on a wall in a museum waiting to be found when you decide you want to find me. This is me. Me with the limp. A war survivor with all the years that helped make me this way. You know what the UN calls us? *Women affected by armed conflict.*"

His mind ran to Katia. The very real Katia at the breakfast table in his apartment in Chicago. To sharing his first journal articles with her, and taking her to meet his mother. Going to the Greek restaurant they liked on Maxwell Street where the waiter knew them and brought them the flaming cheese without having to ask. To them in the shower together. And her laughing that time after the lamp fell off the nightstand as she shook from an orgasm.

Nikoleta looked at him.

"So, tell me about her," she said.

He looked at her.

"My girlfriend?"

"Yes, your girlfriend."

He paused.

"We had just moved in together and I wanted to show her where I was from, and we flew into Zagreb on the way to the coast and I had heard about the museum. And there I was standing like ... I don't know what ... reading the story you wrote about us."

"What is she like?"

"She's lovely. She's Brazilian by birth, adopted by American parents. Smart and patient with me, and passionate and, I don't know what we are now, but we have an apartment in Chicago with all our stuff in it."

Nikoleta nodded.

"And now you're here instead of spending the summer with her?"

He shrugged his shoulders.

"She's in Brazil now, at least I think she's still there. We haven't talked in a couple of weeks. She went to meet her biological family for the first time. She didn't really want me there. Or she knew that I needed to be here. I'm not sure."

They were silent again. He kept fighting off the thought that this was a stupid idea and a waste of an airfare.

"I've read some of your articles," she finally said. "About men and masculinities in the Balkans."

"And?"

"They're good. You see through our men ..."

She said *our* as if it did not include him.

"But?" he said abruptly.

"You write as if you're not from here. As if we were an

exotic tribe you came to study. But you don't write about us like an American casting judgment. You write like you're not from anywhere."

Katia had told him the same thing once; he had gotten defensive and said *that's how you are supposed to write for an academic journal.* That's how you get published, and he was getting published.

"I've read some of your things too," he said. "I Googled you and found a few things you've written."

"And you just left it at that?"

"I didn't know what to say."

She nodded.

"You write passionately about the women, the survivors," he continued. "I saw something you wrote for one of the trials in The Hague and something you wrote about that Dutch soldier who scrawled that shit about Bosnian women."

"I have imagined a special hell for that man."

"When did you leave Bosnia?"

She looked at him with a look that was almost cold.

"After the war. I had an opportunity to study in Canada and that turned into a job with the NGO where I work now. Based in Toronto. It lets me go back and forth, be with my family. The ones who survived the war."

He did not want to face where this might go. Looking at the ground, he was overcome with the feeling of being trapped inside the boundaries of the cement tile square where he stood. He felt he could go nowhere, that he would not be allowed leave, unless he asked for permission.

"Nikoleta, can I ask … I mean …"

He turned away from her.

"Were you raped?" he finally asked, still looking at the ground.

She looked at him; it was disdain mixed with amusement.

"I was lucky," she said, shaking her head, her voice as tense as if she had responded affirmatively. "If lucky is what you can call it."

She paused to light a cigarette before she continued.

"That's what the Americans and Canadians and the rest always want to know. We, my family, were trying to get away from the fighting in Tuzla. We had stopped on the side of the road for a few minutes and the shooting started. I got shot in the hip. Spent weeks in a Serbian hospital. I was immobilized, got a sepsis infection, then had to have a second operation. I survived all that, but was emaciated. My family was working with the Red Crescent at the time trying to get me transferred to the Bosniak side."

She looked at him as if to judge his reaction.

"I had no idea what might happen. I knew the stories, of course, what was happening to women and girls. Once, some soldiers came in to the hospital, drunk, Serbian militia members, looking around. I guess they had taken all the fifteen-year-olds and grandmothers they could find. All their superiors were with the girls in the slave house. They came into my room at the hospital. I was shaking with fear. There was a Serbian nurse who always treated me well. She brought me cigarettes, and wheeled me to a part of the hospital where I could smoke. And sometimes she brought me those Croatian hazelnut chocolates. She didn't say much but she treated me well."

Nikoleta put out her cigarette.

"There were three of them. They had that look. I don't know if you know it. I don't think a man can ever know what that look is. Or maybe you can, they raped and tortured men too. You grew up with them, so maybe you do know the look.

"They stared at me. I could feel the way they looked at me. I think every girl or woman alive knows that look. A man looking at you like you're prey. I knew what was happening. I was silent. The nurse looked back at them saying nothing. She stayed in the room with me even though she had nothing more to do for the night. They asked her what was up with the Bosniak whore. That was me. She told them I was almost killed from a shell to the leg. They laughed and said that that would make me lie still for them."

Goran looked at her, and she at him as if making sure he was paying attention.

"The nurse told them that my wound had gangrene and that I might lose my leg. That she could barely stand the smell of me. Asked them if they knew what gangrene smelled like. The soldiers got this look of nausea on their face. I said nothing, just looked at the floor. They left. I thanked the nurse. She called them pigs. Said that it used to be an officer would court-martial them if they treated a woman like that."

Finally Goran spoke.

"I guess I thought, you know, when I read that you worked for an NGO that helps survivors …"

"That I do this work because I experienced it? That that's what motivates me?"

"Yes."

"In a way. I know the fear that goes with it. But I was lucky."

They had walked around the old part of the city, through a park on what was the Croatian side during the war, and were now circling back toward the bridge. The bridge house hosted a photography exhibit, and

Nikoleta suggested they see it. There were two flights of stairs to climb; Goran watched her ascend, her cane echoing on the wooden steps.

"I never make a quiet entrance," Nikoleta said.

"Does it hurt?" he said, following half a step behind her.

"Not usually. The operations weren't fun but after what so many women went through, I can't complain. This was the best they could make of it considering that all our good doctors left for Germany or Chicago."

He wanted to carry her. He wished it were that simple, that he could simply tell her: *lean into me and let me carry you.*

"What is it?" she asked, feeling his eyes on her.

"Nothing," he said. "I just was thinking about you having to go through that."

"I don't want your pity."

Her look was brutal.

"I don't have any pity to give you. Do you have any for me?" he said, giving her a sheepish smile.

She smiled back; at least he wanted to think it was a smile and not a smirk. They reached the floor with the photos; they showed the bridge during the war, its destruction, and its reconstruction. They both glanced at the photos but they were more engaged in their conversation.

"Any man in your life?" he asked.

"I was with this Canadian guy for a while. I met him during my master's program. I met his family and then he came here with me one time. We were together for almost four years. He's very sweet, but it didn't work out. Maybe I was always thinking about home. Maybe he was too bland for me. Once you have a taste for paprika, you know? Nothing else has flavor."

She smiled. This time he thought it was genuine. He thought maybe it really was that smile, the one from years ago.

Sunset was approaching as they left the photo exhibit, coming down the steps with the same slow pace. The woman at the entrance smiled at them and Goran thought that she and Nikoleta exchanged knowing looks. He had to remind himself that there was no invisible code between survivors of the conflict.

They reached the bridge just about the time the sun was setting. They leaned against the wall.

"My lovely Goran," she said, turning to him. She ran her hand along his cheek and he turned toward her palm, like a cat moving into a stroke. He closed his eyes. "Did you avoid me all these years because you thought I was raped?"

MUSEUM SUBMISSION 31-2008

I had known him since he was a little boy. Our families went to the same church. He was quiet and had a proud face. We both liked to read.

One day, just like that, this small, small boy had become a strong young man. I sat under the tree between our two schools hoping he would notice me. But he looked right through me. I looked at myself in the mirror and thought that I was a small, small girl with nothing to attract him.

Then one day he saw me. He said that I looked different. I had braids and I had started to fill out. And I had a new dress, and that dress fit me in a different way.

He read stories to me and shared his favorite books. We met under the tree every day until he went away to university. While he was away we wrote long love letters. He promised to come back and marry me. I tried not to think about what he might be doing with the girls at university.

We counted the days. I started studying at the teaching college nearby.

It was while he was away at university that the rebel soldiers came. You know what they do. They call this the rape capital of the world.

When he came back, he pretended he did not know me.

I knew why. With women like me, his family would not give him the bride price. I am not a woman he can marry now. No man can.

Here is the first book he gave me. *The Plague*. It is missing the last chapter. When books make it out to us, here in the Kivus, so far from the big cities where they are printed, they are often missing pages. To me, the story ended before Dr. Rieux's wife died. My version ended with the plague having passed its worst stage. We believe things will get better and we think that Dr. Rieux's hard work and bravery will see him through. That he will be rewarded for being virtuous.

I was sad when I learned the real ending.

Some days I wish I could rip out a chapter of my own life just like that. Then maybe those soldiers would never have come. And the big strong boy who liked to read me stories would still be mine.

Goma, Democratic Republic of Congo, 2008

Tyler

Three days later, after he encountered Steven waiting outside the apartment complex, Tyler drove back home after patrol. Sammy was with the babysitter at his apartment. As per routine, Tyler would relieve her and send her on her way. Then they would go have dinner with Joaquin and Carla.

As Tyler pulled up into the apartment complex, the radio in his car was on and a song he liked by a local singer was playing. It had that Austin, indie folk sound, the woman's voice part little-girl and part raspy-sexy in an understated way, the bleak words striking a purposefully ironic pose against her sweet voice:

Seasons change all around me
I keep my ear to the ground
Yeah I know that it's true
What good does it do
Waitin' for the world to end.
Yeah waitin' for the world, waitin' for the world

As he pulled into the parking space, he left the car running for a moment longer so he could hear the end of the song. At one end of the street he noticed what looked like the same truck that he had seen Steven in a few nights before. Carla's car was there as well. If it was his truck, he was not in it. Tyler looked in his rearview mirror and scanned the gate to the apartment buildings to see if he could see Steven.

Turning off the car engine, he pulled his gun and holster out from the glove compartment and put it on. He stepped out of his car and opened the electric gate with his passkey. As it opened, he looked in the direction of Carla's apartment. Her door was closed, and the blinds too. He pulled his T-shirt over his holster, and walked slowly in the direction of Carla's apartment, climbing the stairs in just a few seconds.

He took a deep breath as he knocked on the door. He knew he should call for back-up. Then again, he knew lots of things he should have done that he was not doing lately.

"Carla? Are you home?" he called.

He couldn't see anything through the blinds. He moved back to the door and pulled out his mobile phone and dialed hers. It rang, then went to voicemail.

He knocked on the door again.

"Carla? Joaquin? Are y'all home? Everything okay?" he said.

He turned the doorknob. It was unlocked. He opened the door slowly. It was then that he heard voices from the kitchen, which was around the corner on the other side of the living room.

He told himself there was no reason to walk in with his gun pulled. Joaquin might be inside. It could all be peaceful. He would just have to warn Steven again. He was just checking on them. That was his job. He lifted up his T-shirt slightly, unhitched the holster and unlocked the safety on his gun, resting his hand on it.

"Carla?" he said, taking a step closer to the end of the entryway.

He now had a view of the hallway that led to the bedrooms. Joaquin was walking toward the kitchen, a frightened look on his face. He had apparently not seen

Tyler or was so frightened that he was focused on something else.

"Honey, go back to your room, okay?" Carla said. This was not her normal voice.

"Joaquin, come to your Dad," Tyler heard Steven say.

"Joaquin, stay where you are," Carla said, struggling to sound soothing.

Joaquin stopped at the edge of the kitchen, just inside Tyler's line of sight. He had his back to Tyler and was facing where Tyler guessed Steven and Carla were.

Tyler told himself he should walk in as if he should be there, as if Steven should be there, as if this were all normal and there was no need for alarm.

"Carla? Hey, you home?" he asked, keeping his voice calm as he took the last step to the end of the entryway, where he now had a full view to the kitchen about fifteen feet away.

"Tyler ..." she started.

"Steven," Tyler said, trying to sound as if he were greeting him on any normal day.

"Stay where you are, and keep your hands where I can see them," Steven said, his voice cold and war-zone-stressed-out.

Tyler recognized the tone. He had been in places where men got this weariness and edginess. Tyler kept his hands waist-high, open, palms facing the floor so Steven could see that he wasn't going to do anything with them. Tyler turned his body slightly to hide his gun.

Steven had a pistol. He was restraining Carla's hands behind her back, his left hand big and strong enough to hold both of hers while he held the gun in his right. It was not pointed directly at her but across her and down to the ground. Like all good soldiers, he seemed ready to fire in any direction in a moment's notice. Joaquin stayed at the end of the kitchen, a step away from them.

"Mommy," he whimpered.

"Joaquin, go back to your room, honey," Carla said.

Joaquin didn't move.

"So, our policeman is here," Steven said, aggressively.

"Let's all stay calm," Tyler said, staying where he was, and keeping his hands in the same non-threatening position. "Steven, look, you're violating your restraining order. You know that, right? Now let's just all stay calm and this doesn't have to be a big deal ..."

"Tyler," Carla blurted out.

"Carla, it's okay. We're all gonna be fine. Joaquin, why don't you come over to me?" Tyler said.

"Joaquin. Son. Stay where you are," Steven ordered.

Joaquin did not move. He looked in Tyler's direction for an instant but continued to stand a step away from Carla and from the gun that Steven held in front of her.

"This is something, ain't it?" Steven said, his voice even more menacing. "Guy spends a couple of years of his life surrounded by Taliban and never once fires his gun at 'em yet they send him to protect women."

"Steven, we're all gonna walk away from this, okay? I want you to put your hands out and move away from Carla ..."

"And this asshole of a cop is fuckin' my wife and trying to tell me what to do."

"I'm gonna say it again," Tyler said. "Let's all stay calm and you put your hands out and move away from Carla and Joaquin."

"I don't think you have any authority to be giving orders here," Steven said.

"Mommy," Joaquin whimpered again.

"Joaquin, can you stand back for me?" Tyler said.

"Don't fucking talk to my son like you're his father."

Tyler could see the strain on Carla's face and realized Steven was causing her pain.

"Steven, let's just put the gun down before anyone gets hurt. Joaquin is right here. He's watching all this. Don't make this ..."

He had always thought it an exaggeration when he heard how his fellow officers or soldiers described these moments. That time seemed to move more slowly, that seconds stretched and never seemed to end. Every falling speck of dust and drop of sweat seemed visible and even the faintest sound echoed in a slow reverberation deep in the fear center of the brain.

He had worked so hard to avoid this moment. He had managed to avoid it for so long. At long last Tyler pulled his gun.

It all ran together. Steven shouting *Fuck you*. Carla shouting *Joaquin*. Joaquin crying *Mommy*. Steven's gun in motion. Tyler feeling his gun in his hand, pulling it out and up and pointing it. His finger finding the trigger as if he did this every day. The second hand on the kitchen clock marking another second. A glass crashing in the sink.

There were two shots in rapid succession, followed by a pause and then one more shot, the combined effects leaving that dreaded popping noise bouncing off the thin walls before passing through them.

He felt his adrenaline surge and he looked at the gun in his hand, and though he was moving with all the speed and force in his body, he seemed not to be able to move at all. If they had asked him during the investigation, he would have sworn that in the moment it took him to go from the entryway to the kitchen there was time for a full verse of the song that he had been listening to just a few minutes before it all fell apart.

MUSEUM SUBMISSION 17-1998

Everyone thought the worst part was seeing his body. That part was easy. The waiting was the worst. For months he was missing. *Desaparecido*. Every day they are gone we know they are being tortured. We knew what they did to them. In training they taught us that it was better to be killed than to be caught. It was forty-seven days before we had word.

For seven years I was his *compañera* in the mountains. They don't encourage commanders to have compañeras. But Hector was *indigena*. I'm indigena. They needed us. We make them legitimate. This was our war.

The peace treaty was being negotiated. We could be out in public again. We went to meetings, talked to the UN, gave interviews.

That's when he disappeared. The government said they had

nothing to do with it. They said maybe he was pretending to be *desaparecido*. They said he was *auto-desaparecido*. They said we, the guerillas, did it to make the government look bad.

The UN and the human rights NGOs denounced his disappearance but the government told us nothing. Forty-seven days later, his body was found.

I thought I would be the first one there to see it. I thought it was my right to be the first one. His parents were dead, killed in the conflict. His brother had migrated to the US and his sister was too sad to see anyone.

There was a gringa there when I arrived. Tall and blonde and *flaca* like she didn't eat enough. She knew my name. Her Spanish made her sound like a little girl when she spoke to me.

She was crying when she told me that she had been his *amante*, his lover; when he was traveling for the Movement, or when he was in Mexico in the camps with our refugees. They had a child together, she told me.

When the war was on, when we were fighting, we were always prepared to die, and to mourn our fellow guerrilleros. Every day we knew that could happen. Hector made me tell him that I would leave him behind if I had to, if he were wounded or captured in battle. That I would protect the others and never look back if he was shot. He made me repeat it so many times that I stopped crying. We lost so many comrades that there were not enough tears.

Now I cried. How could I not feel sad that he had this other life, this other family, he never told me about? We spent nights in the mountains, not knowing if we would live through another day. And he met this gringa during the beginning of those years of peace talks. I was with our soldiers in the mountains and he was in conferences, sleeping in clean sheets in hotels. With her. And she had a son with my compañero. And what did I have?

I have this. This picture of him wearing his sash, the one he wore the few times he put on his traditional dress, back in his village before he joined the Movement. It's the kind of weaving that the women from his village used to make. The village that no longer exists. The gringa didn't know that about him. She may have his son, but I have his sash from the village where he was born. Where we have been weaving for longer than her people have been starving themselves to be skinny.

Guatemala, Guatemala, 2007

Goran

After the last sliver of sun went down on the Neretva river, Nikoleta's question—about whether he had avoided her because he thought she had been raped—hung in the air.

"Should I take your silence as a yes?" she asked.

When finally he spoke he couldn't look her in the eyes.

"I avoided you all these years because I felt guilty that I got out and you didn't."

He paused, continuing to look away from her.

"And because for years I believed my father was on the Serbian side that was ... that was ... responsible for all that happened here. I only found out a few years ago that he was one of the Bosnian Serbs who stayed to fight with the Bosniak forces. That he was on the 'right' side. And then I figured out that whichever side he was on, he was still a soldier in a horrible war doing things that we want soldiers to do but we don't want to know about. Of course it matters which side you're on, but no matter what side you're on, it's still a war and you still have to ..."

He stopped for a moment. Maybe it was jet lag and fatigue that led to his honesty; maybe it was that he felt like he was still fourteen and that he was back in the moment when he had just met her. The moment when he was leaving behind everything he knew, when he was nervous and brutally honest because he could be.

"Nikoleta, you were the first real thing for me in my life in Yugoslavia, in Bosnia. Everything else before you and before that moment in the camp was child's play, like a little boy's memories. You were the first and only thing outside of my family that mattered."

He looked at her for a moment and then away; he wanted to see if her eyes still showed anger toward him.

"The truth is I hate most Yugoslavians. I despise the Bosnian or Serbian refugees I meet in Chicago who speak of themselves with an air of superiority that they were able to leave our barbarous past behind us, as if they have nothing to do with what *those people* did to our country. And I hate those other refugees who present themselves as victims to any uninformed American they meet."

He rubbed his hand on his mouth and across the stubble that was beginning to form at the end of the day.

"And the few Yugoslavian intellectuals I know are so removed from it all that they no longer feel anything. They don't have any real connection to it anymore."

He looked at her, then continued.

"I don't know which of those fucking clubs I belong to. I don't want to belong to any of them. But I guess you probably think I'm in the last category."

He repositioned his body against the wall he was leaning on. He looked down at the water below them and then back at her and continued.

"For years I thought you were the only other member of the club I belonged to. I idealized you as the only person who might really understand me. Sometimes I think Katia understands me. She's adopted and African-Brazilian or whatever you would call her, living in a white family, and not sure what club she's in either. But she couldn't get the Balkans part, the Bosnian part of me. That's too much to ask of her."

He turned back to her for a moment and then looked

again at the few lights along both sides of the river bank. He felt her hand on his shoulder. There was nothing more to the hand on his shoulder, no caress, no reaching to him with an offer of redemption, no hint of her wanting more from him. There was just a hand resting on his shoulder.

He could make out faint reflections of light on the water below. There was a long silence, both of them looking at the lights from the darkened bridge, the stars coming out and the lights around them offering enough illumination to see each other. Finally Nikoleta spoke.

"At the beginning of the war, I wondered where the hell you were and why you didn't come for me or contact me. For years, yes, I thought you would come and rescue me. But that doesn't happen, does it? And then I had so many other things to worry about that you just faded after a time—a lovely memory on the bookshelf in my head."

He nodded.

"I meant what I wrote in the museum, that I was sending those things to clean off the shelf and move on. Not from you necessarily but from those first years of the war."

Again, they were both quiet. This time he broke the silence.

"Hey, um, I'm hungry. Would you like to get some dinner and we can ...?" he asked.

"I have to go to my aunt's house for dinner," she said. "There are some cousins coming over whom I haven't seen in a few years."

He waited before saying anything, wondering if she would invite him and wondering what it meant when it became clear that she would not.

"Thursday," she said. "I'll be done with my seminar and

we could spend the afternoon together, before you leave. How is that?"

I am busy. I have a life. I have things I need to get on with. I have Katia, somewhere still, perhaps. I've come all this way just to see you.

"That would be great," he said. "Text me."

"Perfect," she said, and kissed him on the cheek. "I'll see you then. Sorry I have to run, but I'm already very late."

He watched as she half-walked, half-limped away.

Goran dined by himself in an Italian restaurant that his hotel had recommended. He read some local newspapers and took along one of the books he had purchased in Zagreb. The next morning, he took a long run through town, along the river, through a park and then on a few of the busier streets. Back at his hotel he tried for an hour to compose a message to Katia, but he could not think of what to say. Eventually he gave up.

Thursday morning, as promised, Nikoleta texted him, suggesting they meet again at the bridge, at 1:30 p.m.

She was on the bridge before he was and she apparently saw him first, a smile waiting on her lips. He walked toward her and kissed her on the cheek.

"Hey," he said.

"Hey," she said.

She turned and looked in his eyes for a moment and kissed him quickly but purposefully on the lips. He was surprised by this, happily so, and he closed his eyes and moved to kiss her back. There was a charge, an electric current in the kiss. He was sure of it. She moved on as if the kiss had been nothing.

"Let's get something to eat. I left the seminar before the final luncheon and I barely had breakfast. Have you eaten?" she asked.

He opened his eyes and saw her smile, her force, and could only follow.

"No, I haven't."

The lunch conversation was the obligatory catch-up part, the adolescent years, the early adult years, the more recent adult years. The list of people in their lives and where they had gone and what had happened to them after the war. They talked about their work and where they were now: she living in Toronto, he in Chicago; they realized that they were geographically close and that they had even been in each other's cities over the past few years, but had never known.

The sky was a stunning blue in the afternoon. An early morning rain had cleared and the streets had mostly dried. The air smelled as if it had been washed and the limestone walls and old buildings glowed as if freshly scrubbed.

"Shall we go for a walk or maybe a drive? You could show me the countryside," he said. "I haven't driven around here since I was little."

They were sitting across from each other at a small table at an outdoor café, looking onto the river. She reached her hand over to his as the waiter brought their change. He responded, letting his fingers lace with hers. She reached up his arm feeling the skin up to the part where he had rolled up his sleeves.

She leaned in so she could kiss him. This time she meant it. She did not pull away. They were oblivious to the other people in the restaurant, to the tourists, to the waiter—maybe even, for a moment, to all that had come before, to all but that other kiss in the car in the transit camp.

"We can go for a drive tomorrow," she said. "Right now I want you to take me to your hotel room."

❖ ❖ ❖

He kissed her scar. Its center was a thick X and around it were several smaller scars. There was also a thin, jagged scar that wrapped around one side of her ass.

He pulled her underwear all the way off and she leaned back.

Moving from her scars with his tongue, he kissed the rest of her.

She guided him to her. He was tenuous, as if he would hurt her.

"Fuck me. I won't break."

He smiled, obeying her now as he had then.

"Fuck me harder."

He obeyed, her head gently hitting the headboard, his fear that she would break subsiding.

He thought at first that his tears were just fatigue and confusion, but he wasn't sure. Nikoleta looked into his eyes and held his face, smiling gently when she saw that he was crying.

Later, after they slept, he went out and brought back a bottle of wine and some bread, cheese, and fruit for dinner.

Early the next morning, they made love again; this time he needed no instruction. Only later did he think about how effortlessly she moved in bed.

Afterwards she turned to him and, gently kissing him,

said: "I want to show you something."

He nodded, even though he was not sure what she meant. What she wanted to show him was her grandparents' house, the one she had drawn in the picture.

They showered, had breakfast in the hotel dining area, and drove eastward toward the mountains until they reached a small village.

They pulled into a gravel path that had once been a driveway. They looked up at the shell of a brick house, three walls remaining, the roof gone, graffiti scribbled onto some parts, marks from shelling visible. He recognized its shape as the house in the drawing she had sent to the museum. The one she had shown him years ago in the transit camp.

They stepped out of the car. He remained standing by the car, looking at the ruin, making sense of it. The state of the house was as jarring to him as it had been to see Nikoleta limping for the first time. Questions appeared in his head before he asked them out loud. *Did this happen after they left or while they were here? Had they sought refuge?* He waited for her to tell him.

He matched her pace as they walked toward the house, remaining a step behind her.

"I used to play here. We'd come on weekends. Sometimes in the summer or during holidays, I'd stay for weeks, along with my sister and some of my cousins. We would spend hours just roaming, picking flowers, exploring the stream, or helping in the garden. I think I remember all those things. Then other times, I think it could be that I just want to remember all those things.

"It was after my family left, after we tried to get out, right after I tried to give you that drawing I had done of the house. Croatian troops came. My grandparents had already fled. At least they didn't see their house get destroyed."

Goran nodded. Nikoleta was looking away, into the mountains, as she told him this. Clouds had rolled in and the sky took on a menacing tone.

"They had the bad luck of going to Tuzla, where we had family. Who could have known that the Serbian militia would be there first? This was about the same time I was in that hospital."

She looked at him. He felt that she had waited for many years to tell him this story.

"They took the men one direction, to the men's camp, and the women to another. They raped her. Seventy-four years old. A mother of four. Eleven grandchildren."

She paused.

"We always say that rape is not sex, to separate out the sexual desire, which we value and affirm for ourselves as women, right? We separate that from the desire to cause harm and destroy a woman. But I can't help but think that it is sex. That it is men who are having sex. Men with erections. Men who are excited in some way by this. It *is* sex. Men who are so disconnected from their bodies and … I don't know … their souls, if they have them, that they can use their bodies like that."

She looked in the direction of the mountains.

"Why a woman of seventy-four? What possessed these men, young men, to have sex with a woman of seventy-four, a grandmother, someone who in their eyes could be their grandmother?"

She did not expect him to answer.

Goran thought about telling her that he studied these things, men and masculinities and how their country had made them so. But he knew that if he did he would only confirm how much he did not know.

He started to reach out to embrace her, but he could tell that she did not want to be embraced. Her look burned into him.

◆ ◆ ◆

Later, they went back to his hotel and to his surprise, she wanted to make love again. This time, she pulled herself on top of him, used her arms to steady herself, and found a position that was comfortable for her hip.

"Stay right there. There."

Goran moved as commanded. He couldn't tell if she needed this long to reach orgasm or if she wanted to prolong it. She put her hands on his chest, then on top of his shoulders, digging her fingers into them at times as if she wanted to draw him even further into her. He closed his eyes and opened them again as if to confirm that she was really here, with him, like this.

She uttered a sound, a vocalization that transformed into an unspoken declaration. He accompanied her orgasm and wanted to believe that, as she looked in his eyes for the slightest moment and then closed them, she meant it the same way he did.

Afterwards, he gently helped her off, bringing her to his side. He held her and he felt her breathing slow down.

"Chicago and Toronto are not far away," he said. "We could see each other again. I mean be together again ..."

She did not respond. He ran his hands through her hair and thought she might be sleeping. Then, she turned her face toward him.

"Goran, Goran. My dear Goran. Still the boy of fourteen I met in the camp," she said, reaching for his face with a gesture that was more patronizing than tender.

"Is that bad?" he said, smiling.

"No, it's not bad. It's just that I have a life. You have a life. And a girlfriend who loves you. This is ..."

"This is what? Why am I all the way here and you here with me in bed if not ..."

"We're in bed together. You smell good to me. You remind me of a time when my body ached for you. We had good sex. We had a lovely moment years ago in the middle of that hell. We're having a nice moment now. And now we have our lives. We have these memories. Let's not make it more than that. We're not fourteen."

He kept his arm around her but he pulled away slightly. Their bodies were still touching. As these words hit him, something about her smell struck him as acrid.

"You're angry because I didn't come for you sooner," he said. "I didn't come for you years ago when I should have."

"No, Goran, there is no anger. You know that. Not at you. But there is nothing else either. Or maybe there's everything else. There is my life and your life and ... all the things that have happened over the years."

"You said you weren't seeing anyone."

She sighed, then responded, her voice veering toward bitter.

"I have a life in Toronto even if I'm not seeing someone. I can't uproot all I've made for myself and my life in Toronto just for two afternoons of good sex."

"I'm not asking you to move to Chicago and uproot yourself. I'm just saying, we could see each other."

"Goran, go home. You're not from here anymore. Just because you remember some colorful curses, your Bosnian is still good, you like burek, and you remember those moments at the beginning of the war, doesn't mean you're still Bosnian. Come visit me in Toronto if you want. I'll meet you for coffee or dinner. Maybe we'll fuck again."

He inhaled.

"Maybe what I need is someone who has no connection with any of this," she continued. "Who can make me laugh and make me forget. Who has none of this in his past and doesn't expect me to help him understand it. Who doesn't feel like he owes me anything."

He was silent, letting his chin rub against her shoulder and letting his hand rest against her thigh. There was part of him that wanted to stay here, to memorize her and the feel of her skin and every part of her. And part of him that felt he had simply tumbled into a strange bed with a drunken hookup the night before. And that he needed to get back to somewhere, or someone, who felt like home.

They showered and dressed and he walked her to the bridge. She asked more about Katia along the way but she was perceptive enough to tell by his two-word responses that he was not interested in talking about her, or in talking at all.

"You've become a fine man, Goran. I don't mean to sound arrogant, like it's my job to judge or something. That's just my opinion, from someone who met you years ago when you were still a boy."

He nodded. He reached out for her hand and pulled it to his mouth, kissing her palm and then holding it to his cheek for a short moment. Her words struck him as strange. They were words he had needed and wanted to hear for many years but now they felt stale, their expiration date long since passed.

A thousand desperate measures and words ran through his head. For a moment he thought she could read them all, could see them all in his eyes.

"Stay well," she said.

"You too," was all he could respond as he released her hand and she turned to walk away.

He turned back to watch her unsteady walk. She did not turn for one last look at him. She cleared the bridge and turned a corner. He remembered that day in the transit camp when she invited him to follow her to the empty car at the rear of the school. This time, he did not run after her.

He stayed in the same place on the bridge, leaning against the railing. Everything was buzzing and burning in his head and he could not decide where he should go or how he would get there.

He listened to the voices around him, all Bosnian, using expressions he remembered and understood, that reminded him of the time before the war. He smelled the familiar, pungent cigarette smoke. There were families, men and women by themselves or with children, children walking alone or in small groups, talking and laughing, walking on the rebuilt bridge that was still a lifeline that connected the two sides of the city. As he listened in on the conversations, he could finish phrases. Goran knew the punchline to the joke that one boy was telling to another about the policeman with no money who goes to the whorehouse. He recognized all the terms of endearment he heard parents using with their children. The smell of *ćevapi* being cooked in a restaurant nearby was as familiar as his Chicago apartment.

Goran realized in that moment, as the emptiness of her departure faded, that he had somewhere to be and something to do. He was not yet done here. Nikoleta was right in saying that he was not from here anymore, and probably never would be again, but he had unfinished Bosnian business.

◆ ◆ ◆

It was early afternoon by the time he reached Sarajevo the next day. He returned the rental car at the airport.

Then he took a taxi into town and checked into a simple hotel.

As soon as he put his bag down, he looked at his phone. He had registered the number as *Otac*. Father. He pressed "Call." His father picked up on the second ring.

"It's me, Goran."

There was a slight pause. Just before he was about to repeat himself, his father spoke.

"Hello, Goran." And then a pause. "What do you want?"

"There is more I want to know, Otac. We didn't finish the last time I was here."

For a moment Goran thought his father might have walked away from the phone or hung up.

"Ok, Goran. I will tell you more. Anything you want to know."

"I'm in Sarajevo."

"Yes, good. That's good. Let's go drinking. When is good for you, my son?" his father said.

"Yes, drinking. Around 7 p.m.," Goran responded.

MUSEUM SUBMISSION 8-1-2012

I don't know how you prepare anyone to lose a child. My parents, my adopted parents, lost their first love. A baby boy. I cannot fathom my father having to watch the motorcycle hit him. How does your mind even prepare you for that? I find it obscene even to describe it. I feel disgust that I have been to the street where it happened and that I have that image in my head. I apologize for sharing it with you now. But it's part of my story.

My father lives with that memory every day and remembers every night that he let go of my brother's hand.

They adopted me right after that. I was a newly orphaned baby girl. It was in Rio de Janeiro. I was their substitute baby, or something like that. They took me back to the US, where they are from.

Years later, as you can probably guess, I went back to find my biological family. I could tell you the full story of my mother falling in love with a drug dealer from a rival gang to the one her brother, my uncle, was in, but that's all you need to know to guess how that story ended. They set her on fire. She was eight months pregnant with me and despite her injuries she lived until a week after I was born.

On my roots trip, I found my Brazilian grandmother. She lives on a small farm in the rural Northeast of Brazil. As she held me, grateful to see me alive and healthy, I should have embraced being Brazilian. I so wanted to.

I wanted to look at this dress and think about my mother being killed by my father and think that she was heroic and willing to die for love, for him and for her brother. That she willed herself to live long enough to give birth to me.

But when I opened this yellowed box, and when I saw that it was the burnt remains of her wedding dress, all I felt was that I wanted to be rid of it. I didn't want it in my hands or in my house and I didn't want to smell the faint odor of mildew and the poverty that it reminded me of.

Am I horrible for thinking that?

And I couldn't tell my grandmother that I hated the lullaby she said my mother sang to me. It didn't sound like a song I would ever sing to a baby. It sounded like a funeral dirge and I thought why would you sing a funeral dirge to a baby?

Before I left my grandmother's farm I thought that I wanted her to teach me how to make Brazilian food or some medicine from plants or something that would affirm that I was from there, that I was African-Brazilian from a rich tradition. But I didn't.

Right then, I just wanted to leave. And I knew exactly where I wanted to be.

I was twelve years old and I looked different to them of course, but I was just the black girl on the street. I was the black girl with the white parents and it was all normal. And I didn't know yet how my biological mother was killed or how my brother died. The twelve-year-old me came home from school everyday and I knew without a doubt that my parents loved me.

I want that back. That is my lost love. That moment of being a twelve-year-old girl loved by her parents and knowing little of what came before and nothing of what would come after.

Rio de Janeiro, Brazil, and Austin, Texas, 2012

Tyler

It was Tyler's mother who had read about the traveling exhibition. It came from a museum in Europe—a museum where people sent stories of lost and broken love. She had seen an article about it in the Houston newspaper. It would be in Austin at the University of Texas museum for the next two months.

His mother thought it would be good for him. She suggested he send in a story about Carla, his story with Carla. It might help him, she said.

Although more than a year had passed, he could not find the words to write about her. He was never all that good at writing down his feelings anyway. But he was curious about the stories of others, about the kinds of stories people would send in, and he was pleased to have a few hours without the two boys, and without his classroom full of restless and sweaty twelve-year-olds.

He read every one of the museum entries. He let the words and the voices fill his mind. For the first time in months he was not in a hurry. His mother was with the boys and she told him to take his time.

This visit to the exhibition was the first time in months that he'd had time to think. After Carla was killed, Joaquin had stayed with Carla's mother for a few months and Sammy and Tyler had visited him regularly. On one of those visits, Carla's mother had told Tyler about her kidney condition. She would need dialysis for the rest of her life. She had discussed it with her other daughter and they both wanted to know if Tyler would consider adopting Joaquin. She felt sure Joaquin would like the idea.

Tyler had nodded.

And then the social worker from the state child welfare agency asked him what he thought about the idea.

Again Tyler nodded.

"I'd like that. I'd be happy with that. Sammy would too."

And so, Tyler became a father of two.

Tyler had come early for the opening day of the exhibition. It was a Saturday morning. They were serving snacks and champagne and Tyler had taken a glass. He read the entry about the woman in Jamaica, and the young man in the seminary, and then he came upon a story that made him linger. It was the one about the woman who was originally from Rio de Janeiro and adopted by an American couple.

As he finished reading, he took a deep breath. He could feel grief roll into him again, bringing with it the moment when Carla was killed. He took another breath.

He looked away from the entry and to his left a few steps behind him; he sensed someone looking at him. There was an African-American woman who looked familiar. He breathed deeply and slowly.

"Tyler?" she said.

"Katia, I mean Ms. Baum," he responded.

"Katia is fine. I'm so sorry about what happened. I heard, of course ..." she said. "How is Sammy?"

"He's great. Actually, I have two now. Carla's son, Joaquin, is living with us now. The adoption will be finalized in a few months."

He could read the confusion in her eyes. He had seen this reaction before. How *does* one respond to the act of taking in a murdered woman's son? *Congratulations? I'm so sorry?*

"They must be about the same age, aren't they?"

"Yup, two five-year-olds who act like they take Red Bull intravenously."

She smiled.

"Are you still on the police force?"

For a moment he had to remind himself that he was not in a therapy session with her, and that her questions were just the stuff of conversation. He could stand here next to her, talk to her, smile at her, look at her, even imagine asking her out.

"No, gave that up. I just finished my teacher certification and I'm doing the student teaching placement to become a sixth-grade history and social-studies teacher. So, twelve-year-olds during the day and five-year-olds the rest of the time."

She nodded, and looked at him with the warm smile he remembered.

"It's a great idea, these stories," he said.

She nodded.

"Did you see the one from Brazil? The woman ..." he said.

He pointed to the glass case with a small black pendant of a fist and the charred remains of a dress.

Her look turned serious.

"That's me," she said.

He stared at her for a long moment; now it was his turn to be confused about how to respond. He turned away, as if looking back at the exhibit, and the small fist, and then back to her.

"Wow. I'm ... I don't know what to say."

"Yeah. I learned all the details of how it happened last year. I went to Brazil to meet my biological grandmother."

"So you're Brazilian but you spent your whole life here?"

"Yeah. Adopted by a family from Madison, Wisconsin. About as American as it gets."

He looked over at the space where Katia's letter was on the wall, and then back at Katia. She looked at him. It could have been awkward standing there, with this relative stranger, but it was not. It felt comfortable just standing here with her.

"Tyler, do you mind if I ask about what happened when ... I had hoped you might come see me after all that."

"Yeah, I know. I thought about coming to see you but it was just so busy ... I've been reliving it in my head for more than a year and I've come to figure out that it's about coming to terms with it. Forgetting it doesn't seem to be an option."

She nodded.

"You shot him ..."

"No. No."

"Oh, I thought I read ..."

"He shot her and then he turned his gun on himself."

She looked at him now, as if to gauge whether he could take any more of these questions. He told her how it happened.

Katia looked at him. It was a look that made him feel comforted and cared for without feeling pitied. He was about to say more, maybe to ask her if she wanted another champagne. Or if she might meet him for a coffee some time. Not as a therapist.

It took him a moment to register that the man coming up to them was someone who knew her.

"Hey," Katia said, to the man, and took his hand in

hers. "Tyler, this is Goran. Goran, this is Tyler Nielsen. Tyler used to be on the police force in Bastrop and was assigned to guard the women's shelter there. Remember the incident about the woman there who was killed by her ex-husband? Tyler was her ... um, boyfriend."

"Oh, man. So sorry to hear that. Last year, wasn't it?"

"Yup," Tyler said.

The way Katia looked at Goran and reached for his hand made it obvious to Tyler that there was affection and intimacy between them of a deep and enviable kind.

"Are you still a police officer?" Goran asked.

"No, not anymore," Tyler said. "Not after that. And not after I, well, adopted her son. I had my own son already, and with two boys to care for, being a police officer just didn't make sense."

Goran and Katia nodded.

"You live in Austin?" Tyler asked, looking at Goran.

"I teach in Chicago but I'm hoping to move here in a few months," Goran said.

Tyler saw the look of complicity between the two of them as he said this.

Behind them, a voice crackled over a PA system. Tyler didn't pay attention to it except to hear that one of the founders of the Croatian museum was about to speak.

"Well, it was good to see you Katia, and good to meet you," Tyler said, looking first at Katia, then at Goran, and reached to shake their hands.

"The boys are lucky to have you, Tyler," Katia said, hanging on to his hand for just a moment longer than he expected.

Their eyes met briefly and then they disconnected their gazes as he turned to move through the exhibition space.

He passed by the objects on the wall again. The work

gloves. The perfume bottle. The flask for semen collection. The tattered cover of *The Plague*. The *figa*. He examined the last exhibit. It was a shiny tennis trophy sent by a woman whose boyfriend died before things really even got started for them. He thought about Joaquin's Big Wheel tricycle sitting outside Carla's apartment and that first time Sammy walked over to it.

He stepped out of the coolness of the university museum and into the hot Central Texas air. He walked in the direction of the parking garage, thinking about seeing the boys. He thought about the sweaty, incessant energy that swirled around him when the three of them were together.

Tyler wondered about all the letters and objects that didn't make it into the exhibition. He imagined a colossal warehouse filled with them. He thought of the rejected objects and the letters in the warehouse; he imagined it was difficult to choose which ones to exhibit.

Tyler pulled his aviator sunglasses from his shirt pocket and put them on. He reached in his pocket for his keys.

For a moment, as he walked the rest of the way to his car, as he thought about all the stories, the ones on display and the ones in a warehouse somewhere, he felt he was part of something. Something as big and real and endless as the pale, cloudless, arid Hill Country sky above him. Something as concrete as the eight-lane Interstate highway that would take him home to the two boys who called him Daddy.

Acknowledgments

John Crownover and Nakto Geres first took me to the museum that partly inspired these stories. Both of them indulged me when I wanted to go back to the museum a second and a third time. They also introduced me to the amazing, messy place that is the former Yugoslavia. Natko provided the translation and taught me everything I know about Balkan cursing. Thanks also to Vojkan Arsic, Adnan Cviko, and Sasa Petkovic for sharing their personal stories. They have patiently responded to my many questions about Yugoslavian life and history over the years I have had the honor of working with them.

For comments and encouragement along the way, my deepest thanks to Michael Kaufman, my brother-in-writing and ever-thoughtful critic. Thanks also to Simone Ratzik, Alyse Bass, Paul Bloem, Maddy Wilkes, Andrew Levack, Henny Slegh, and Ruben Zonenshein for their comments on early versions of the manuscript. And thanks to my daughter Nina, whose keen sense of social justice keeps me aware and questioning at all times. My parents, Phyllis Barker and Robert Barker, live in the real-life town of Bastrop, Texas, and helped in countless ways. My thanks to Paul Buckley and Lydia Unsworth for their insightful and astute edits and comments. And to Judith Uyterlinde for these years of support and guidance.

Finally, to my partner, Suyanna, for her patience and generosity in reading, listening, critiquing, and discussing. And for inspiring me always to write, and to write intensely and honestly. When she likes the story, it is her delight that fills me.

10-18-19
3-10-22
<u>ℛ (LHQ)</u>
10/28/21
4

On the Design

As book design is an integral part of the reading experience, we would like to acknowledge the work of those who shaped the form in which the story is housed.

Tessa van der Waals (Netherlands) is responsible for the cover design, cover typography, and art direction of all World Editions books. She works in the internationally renowned tradition of Dutch Design. Her bright and powerful visual aesthetic maintains a harmony between image and typography and captures the unique atmosphere of each book. She works closely with internationally celebrated photographers, artists, and letter designers. Her work has frequently been awarded prizes for Best Dutch Book Design.

The image on the cover is taken by Diana Bejarano, a photographer and artist from Bogotá, Colombia living in NYC. It comes from a series entitled 'My White Dress' and is inspired by the Brides' March against domestic violence, an annual march through the streets of New York that began in 2001. The dresses Bejarano photographed were donated by marchers, and intend to serve as canvases that embody the stories of women who have been victims of domestic abuse. Bejarano is interested in developing projects within communities and working with NGOs to question perceptions and help us connect to each other. The photograph has been colored to add a vibrancy and emotion in keeping with the novel's themes.

The cover has been edited by lithographer Bert van der Horst of BFC Graphics (Netherlands).

Suzan Beijer (Netherlands) is responsible for the typography and careful interior book design of all World Editions titles.

The text on the inside covers and the press quotes are set in Circular, designed by Laurenz Brunner (Switzerland) and published by Swiss type foundry Lineto.

All World Editions books are set in the typeface Dolly, specifically designed for book typography. Dolly creates a warm page image perfect for an enjoyable reading experience. This typeface is designed by Underware, a European collective formed by Bas Jacobs (Netherlands), Akiem Helmling (Germany), and Sami Kortemäki (Finland). Underware are also the creators of the World Editions logo, which meets the design requirement that 'a strong shape can always be drawn with a toe in the sand.'